The AUKUS Enigma

A Novel

By

C.W. Lumpkin

And

S.R. Gibson

Table of Contents

Chapter One

The Pentagon

SecNav (Secretary of the Navy) sat at the head of the conference table. Seated around the table were Admiral Hanover and the top brass of the United States Navy and behind each officer was one chair for their aides, most were empty.

The SecNav cleared his throat. "Gentlemen, there has been a breach of top secret information from the AUKUS deal. It was announced worldwide in the press and revealed that the US and the UK are sharing nuclear submarine technology with Australia." He looked around the crowed room.

He referred to some notes. "The US and UK are to provide aid to integrate the technology into a new Australian class sub because the Chinese are blatantly sending their ships into the South Pacific and openly intimidating the Aussie navy. That is unacceptable."

Those seated at the table began to look at each other. The fact that the nuclear technology would be shared with Australia was now public knowledge. What was so bad about that?

One of the men seated was obviously not military. The SecNav pointed at the civilian. "Gentlemen, Mike Donovan is with the CIA. His function is to coordinate with NCIS and oversee an investigation into who leaked the agreement to the press." That brought some raised eyebrows. Some stared at Donovan with steely eyes. SecNav nodded at Donovan.

Donovan stood, "Gentlemen, this is a disaster." Eyes rolled. "The press had the facts before any of our intelligence organizations knew what was happening." Donovan read an article from the Australian press.

On Thursday morning Australian time, with Morrison [Prime Minister of Australia] in Canberra, Johnson [Prime Minister UK] in London and Biden [President of US] in Washington, the [Aussie Prime Minister] dumped one good friend [The French], threw his lot in with another, [Biden], who appeared to the entire world like he couldn't remember the name of "that fella down under".

No one made a comment about the article.

The French were very underwhelmed, with Defense Minister Jean Le Dread saying: "The AUKUS deal was made while we were bent over. They gave it to us in the backside."

Some around the table knew, it's was a Larry, Curley and Moe moment.

Canberra, Australia

The meeting was called quickly. No one had a clue what it was all about. Lt. Randolph Brice sat in silence as the Vice Admiral told all the staff how the Covid-19 virus had hit all Australian ships with devastation. Some in the room knew they would be seconded to various ships to assist them to maintain as much presence in Australian waters as possible, not that there was an eminent threat. At least Lt. Brice hoped not.

Brice had been in the RAN (Royal Australian Navy) for six years, but never on a ship. He didn't think they were going to put him on a ship. He hated ships. *Everyone knows I get seasick.*

"Brice, you are to report to the HMAS Robertson."

Oh crap. He looked up when his name was called. A young seaman rushed to him with a large envelope. She smiled and handed him the package as if it was going to explode and hurried back to her desk.

The Admiral kept reading names. Brice tuned him out.

He looked at the name typed on the label hoping there has been some horrible mistake, nope, it read Lieutenant Randolph Brice.

He opened the package and read the first page.

Name: LT. R. Brice Assignment: HMAS Robertson Perth
Duty starting: September 6th.

He looked at his cell phone. It displayed the date as August 30th. He was in Canberra. Perth is on the other side of the freaking country. I have never been to Perth. How the hell am I supposed to get to Perth? What kind of ship is the HMAS Robertson?

The second sheet stated the ship was a destroyer class war ship. Brice thought that sounded good. The third sheet says he is to replace the tactical officer. He knew what a tactical officer's job was supposed to do, but it required extensive training and months of hands on experience. Brice had never been on the bridge of a war ship or any other kind of ship.

He dug around in the envelope and found reservations on a Royal Australian Air Force plane leaving Canberra on September 4th, arriving in Perth on September 5th. He was stunned. It will take a jet two days to get there. Then he saw the take off time is 2100.

In the back of the room stood a man in a tan rain coat with the collar turned up, Bogart style. It was not raining. He spoke into his cell phone.

Beijing, China

Science Officer Chi Lu Chong sat in a boring meeting. The Admiral was explaining the fleet's new mission in the South Pacific. Chong had recently completed two years of intense training on nuclear and propulsion detection systems, a top secret area. He had been promoted to a fleet

Science officer only 8 days ago and had no idea what this meeting was all about.

He jerked his head up when he heard his name called as the Admiral read off duty assignments. Chong was assigned to one of China's latest and most secret nuclear submarines. He had never been on a sub. He hated small spaces and broke out in hives most of the time. He squirmed in his seat.

An Officer delivered a fat envelope with his orders. Chong's hands were trembling, holding the envelope as if it contained a deadly virus. He never imagined he would be on a submarine. He thought science officers worked in labs a long way from the ocean. The Admiral told the group that individual instructions would be given later, one on one. Sweat was pouring down his forehead and his hands shook.

The meeting broke up. Chong stood at attention as the Admiral and his staff left the meeting room. Many of the people who had received orders were smiling and slapping each other on the back. Chong was not one of them.

A man in civilian clothing, with a fedora like a mafia boss, stood quietly in the back observing the group. His attention was focused on Chong.

London, England

Commodore Edsel Thomas was all business. In a loud voice, he began dishing out assignments to his senior officers.

"Gentlemen, it seems, someone has leaked some top secret information about the US and

UK's agreement to share nuclear information regarding submarines with Australia."

Not everyone looked surprised. Those with top secret clearance knew the arrangements were made over eight months ago. The others looked around for some clue as to what the Admiral was talking about.

"The French had assumed Australia would use the French design and purchase the sub from them. The estimated cost was 90 billion. The work on the new class of submarine is being done at the top secret Adelaide boat works, in South Australia. We sent three of our top nuclear submarine experts to Australia to oversee the secret construction.

"The Yanks sent three of theirs from, New London, Connecticut. Things were going on schedule when suddenly the press dropped the bomb. The entire Intelligence community has been caught off guard."

A murmur came from the group. Finger pointing began. The Admiral abruptly ordered half the UK fleet from the Indian Ocean to the waters around Australia. No one understood why. Was there a threat?

Colonel McClusky of MI-6 stood in the back. He adjusted his rain coat even if it wasn't raining. This was right down his alley. He was ordered to start the hunt for the leaker. It was not known how or why the information was leaked. The Foreign office was embarrassed. That meant a lot of cover-up and misinformation that would muddle up the hunt.

Toulon, France

François DePaul received a call at 0500. The caller instructed him to report to the French Navy's headquarters at 1000.

At 1000 sharp, DePaul stepped out of the elevator. Eight naval officers were milling about waiting for something. There were several armed sailors standing in front of the double doors leading into a meeting room. DePaul was not given specific instructions. He had no idea what his summons here was about.

"Francois, I'm surprised to see you here," said a tall middle aged man in a commodore's uniform.

Francois turned and smiled. The man was his brother-in-law and a real stick in the mud. "Yes, I'm as surprised as you. Do you know what is going on?"

The man looked at Francois and smiled. "This meeting is top secret and only for those with top secret clearance." The smug look told Francois his brother-in-law was trying to insinuate he was not qualified to be at the meeting, whatever it's for. Francois was one of France's top secret agents with a code name of Kluso. His brother-in-law had no idea what he did. He thought Francois was a clerk in the Navy operations department.

An Admiral and two of his staff stepped from the elevator. Francois recognized the Admiral as the French Navy's top fleet commander. He had secretly worked on the Admiral's strategic planning staff a year ago before being selected to attend special training classes.

The Admiral spotted DePaul and walked up. Francois saluted. "Francois, I'm glad you are here." Francois made no attempt to introduce his brother-in-law. The Admiral turned and motioned for one of his staff to step forward. "Sergeant, please give Francois a packet."

The brother-in-law suddenly found an interest in another group of officers and joined them. He kept his eyes on Francois and the Admiral. He was shocked at his brother-in-law's relationship with the Admiral on a first name basis.

A man in civilian clothes asked all to follow him into the conference room. They filed in and were seated. The Admiral and his staff took their seats. Most were looking for the Admiral to start the meeting. There was dead silence. Several minutes went by. Eyes were shifting from one to the other.

The door banged open and three people entered the room. The Prime Minister along with two body guards marched to the head of the table. The PM stood behind a podium. Missing was the French Minister of Defense. The PM's face was red and it was quite obvious he was not happy.

"Gentlemen, I am pissed off. It seems France has once again been kicked to the back benches by the UK and the Yanks. No one in the room had a clue what he was talking about.

He went on to explain. "The Australians presumably purchased the latest of our submarines. They [Aussies] halted construction seven months ago shortly after it was started. Not one word as to why. Then we learn from the damn world press, who evidently have better spies than we do, why." DePaul moved uneasily in his seat.

"The UK and the Yanks have decided to share their nuclear technology for submarines with the Aussies. Not even our best intelligence saw this happening. We cannot let this happen. The cost to our economy will be huge. We must find a way to make sure the Aussies buy our technology." Everyone looked at the PM as if he had announced everyone had been assigned to North Africa.

Adelaide

A rubber dingy was lowered over the side of a Chinese submarine at 1900. The sun had set but it was not completely dark. A crewman placed a box of fish, bait and fishing tackle into the rubber boat. One man dressed in fisherman's gear climbed down the rope ladder and started the small outboard motor.

The craft slowly moved away from the sub. The sub immediately submerged. The entire exercise took less than three minutes.

It was at least ten kilometers to the shore. The sea was calm and the lights of the city could be seen clearly coming on. In Fifty minutes the rubber dingy pulled up to the wharf with many other fishing boats already tied up. Only a few men were still working on their boats.

Lee picked up his box of fish and sat them on the wooden wharf. A fish monger walked to the box and picked up a fish. He looked back at the fisherman. "Don't see many of these. Where were you when you snagged this lot?"

Yen Lee looked up as he climbed the stairs with his gear. "Out quite a ways, I Lost track of time. I hope I'm not taking someone's place. I don't normally come this way, but the darkness got me. I usually sell my lot at Maslin." His English was perfect, even a slight Aussie accent.

The monger smiled. Well you're in luck; no one uses this tie up. I'll give you Three dollars a kilo." He looked at Lee. Lee was shaking his head no. "Okay, five dollars and that's it.

Lee smiled and said, "Deal." The man moved the box to the scales and poured the fish into the basket. The weight came to eighteen kilos. He counted out ninety dollars and poured the fish back in the box. "Nice doing business with you. If you come back this way again, tie up here and I'll do a deal with you. I haven't seen this type of fish in months." He waved at a heavy set man to come get the box.

Lee pocked the money and picked up his tackle. He looked carefully around; no one seemed to notice him. He made his way to the street and walked to the hotel his handler had arranged for a room. He checked into his room. He watched a channel 7 news show and then turned in for the night.

The next day, Yen Lee went to the fish wharf. He found the man that bought his fish and offered to sell his rubber boat for a very low price. The man paid him and he headed for the boat works and applied for a job. His union papers stated he was a master welder. The boat works needed as many master welders as it could hire. There was always an opening. He was interviewed and his papers were examined. The interviewer made two calls. The MSS had hacked into the labour union database and entered all the info required for Yen Lee to appear as a union master welder. He was hired and would start work the next day. He thought it would have been much harder.

Chapter Two

Perth, Australia

The RAAF jet taxied to the small passenger terminal at Pearce military airport in Western Australia. From his window, Brice could see lots of people doing their jobs, stacking boxes and baggage onto carts. The jet braked to a stop. The door opened and stairs were pushed to the opening.

He got up from his seat and got in the queue to deplane. There were only twenty or so passengers.

He walked down the long stairs to the tarmac. The temps were comfortable, in the upper twenties, a beautiful spring morning. His bag was waiting on the tarmac at the bottom of the stairs.

Brice grabbed his bag and followed everyone to the terminal. He had no clue what to do. No one gave him any instructions. A young man in a Hawaiian shirt holding a cardboard sign with his name crudely scribbled on it. Duh! He was the only person wearing a Navy Uniform in the building. Brice nodded at him and walked over to where he was perched on top of a baggage cart.

"Hello, I'm Lieutenant Brice." He sailor looked behind Brice as if to make sure there wasn't anyone else named Brice.

"Sir, I'm to take you to the ship and assist you with anything to assure your comfort." Brice thought, *Wow, a personal attendant. That was unexpected, but hey, this is all new to me.* "What is your name?" He hopped down off the cart.

"I am Seaman first class Elroy McDuffie. I'm from Townsville, Queensland." Brice looked at his attire, which would have been perfect for Hawaii. Oh well, maybe this is normal for Perth.

"Well Seaman McDuffie, let's get going. I only have this one bag." The seaman looked at Brice like someone would look at a six year old going to camp for the first time. He reached down and picked up the duffle bag.

They walked a hundred meters to a car park. A shiny new navy jeep was parked in a reserved spot. Brice thought, *wow, I'm getting the royal treatment.*

They walked right past the new jeep. Brice looked down the row of vehicles; there was what looked like an old rusty Moke [Dune Buggy] discarded twenty years ago from Magnetic Island off the coast of Townsville, Queensland.

The seaman threw Brice's duffle into the rear seat that had badly cracked upholstery with springs sticking out. There was no boot. The steering wheel was on the Yank side. Brice went around to the other side and climbed in. No seat belt. No windscreen.

McDuffie climbed in and turned the key. Nothing happened. He jumped out and flipped his seat back. The battery was under his seat. It looked like it had fur growing out of the terminals. He jiggled the cables and put the seat back. He reached in and pulled a dirty towel from the glove box and wiped his hands and climbed back in. He turned the key. It fired up. He smiled and away we went.

The HMAS Robertson

They entered the port area. Brice was amazed at the number of ships tied up. He looked down the rows and tried to identify his ship, HMAS Robertson. Without warning, Seaman McDuffie turned off the main road onto a semi paved road that ran parallel with the bay. It was more like an abandoned road. The holes were big enough swallow a tank. They hit one deep enough to jar his teeth. In the distance was a lone ship tied up at a dilapidated wooden wharf.

The closer they came to the ship the more he thought that can't be an active ship. The poor thing has more patches than a quilt. It's listing to the starboard side at least ten degrees and the bridge seemed to have huge red painted blotches. The closer they got he saw it was not paint but pure rust.

A large number 54 was painted on the bow. The numbers were nearly unreadable. The rust had nearly consumed the 5. The deck gun was turned at an odd angle. He looked at McDuffie, hoping he was playing a practical joke. McDuffie looked straight ahead.

"Seaman, is that the Robertson?" He looked at Brice like one would a homeless dog.

"Yes sir. The Captain brought us here from Adelaide for repairs. The boat works in Adelaide said they couldn't fix her. The works here said they would give it a go, but didn't promise anything."

"Have the repairs been completed?"

"No sir. We are not on the high priority list."

"When did you arrive?"

"Last June." Holy crap, the ship has been tied up here since last June.

"What is wrong with the ship? Is it sea worthy?"

"Sir, I think you need to speak to the Captain about that. I don't know."

Brice looked closer as they arrived at the bottom of the decaying wharf. There were four men dressed in jeans and T-shirts standing in the shade of a lean-to that was on the verge of falling down.

When they arrived, the four standing in the shade looked over and jumped to attention. Lt. Brice returned their salute. They looked at each other. One held out his hand, the others put a few bank notes in the offered hand. Brice thought w*hat had they bet on? Whatever it was, they seemed okay with the outcome.*

Seaman McDuffie pulled the bag out from the back seat. "Sir, follow me and I will show you to your cabin and meet the Captain."

He looked over at the four seamen and asked, "The Captain?" They all shrugged their shoulders. The two climbed the boarding ramp. It was full of holes where you could see the water below. It squeaked and sagged as they climbed. He was afraid the thing would collapse before they reached the ship.

McDuffie stepped onto the deck, turned and saluted a flag flapping on the stern. It looked like it had seen its best days. The Chief Boson's Mate, who had a cigarette dangling from his mouth, sat on a crate with a clip board. One of the men standing next to the Chief got a swift elbow in the ribs. The man jumped and started fumbling to find his pipe. He finally found it and blew four tweets. It sounded like a bagpipe gone south. The Chief Boson's Mate made a grimace and turned to the new arrivals. "You must be Lieutenant Brice?"

Brice stared at him, and nodded yes. He looked at his clip board. "Well that's it for today." He made a move to leave.

Brice stood looking at a bad case of discipline. "Seaman, attention, and salute your superior officer." He flipped the cigarette overboard and looked at Brice for a few seconds, stood and saluted. They faced each other on a ten degree slanted deck. Brice saluted back. They heard a hatch open and bang against the steel bulkhead. The Chief smiled and sat back down on the crate. McDuffie tapped Brice on the shoulder. "Sir this is Captain Raines."

Captain Raines

The man was dead drunk. His uniform appeared to have been slept in for weeks and the man had at least a four day beard growth. Brice could smell his stale breath from two meters away.

"Who the hell are you?" Brice was stunned. This must be Captain Bligh and I'm Mr. Christian.

He saluted. The Captain stood staring at him. He leaned against the bulkhead, most likely to keep from falling, and looked Brice over as a loud burp came from his mouth. "You here to replace Gonzales?"

"I don't know sir. I was assigned here to replace the tactical officer." Everyone looked at each other and began to snicker, which soon turned into a downright laugh fest.

"Son, I think you found the right ship, but we need a tactical officer like a third eye." Hic, "McFuddddy, show the Lieutenant to his luxury suite." Everyone heehawed. Brice was beginning to think he was assigned to the HMAS Jokester. McDuffie did not seem to mind his name being mispronounced.

The Lieutenant followed McDuffie through a series of hatches and down steep stairs, more like ladders. They stopped in front of a door labeled, LT. Gonzales. The bulb in the wall fixture must have burned out. It was dark and spooky. Brice squinted to see the name.

"Sir we'll have your name on the door by tomorrow. We had to make sure someone actually showed up." He opened the door, which shrieked loudly from rusty hinges, and attempted to pull down the bunk from the niche in the wall. After several tries, it finally plopped in place. He threw the duffle bag on the bunk. The cabin was smaller than Brice's closet in Canberra. "Sir, have a good day." With that, McDuffie saluted and disappeared down the corridor.

Brice closed his door. The rusty hinges made a noise that would wake the dead. He'd have to get some oil on those hinges. He began to examine his room. It was compact. A head [Toilet], fold down desk, a fold down bunk, a book shelf with one book, 'How to be a Tactical Officer for dummies', one fold down seat, and a closet that would hold no more than two or three uniforms.

He stood in his clean white officer's uniform. He didn't want to touch anything, but the room looked clean, although he was afraid he'd get rust stains on his uniform from brushing against the bulkheads. Rust would never come out.

He emptied his duffle bag onto the bunk and selected fatigues. He carefully hung up his clean white uniform.

Exploration of the HMAS Robertson

Brice decided to explore the ship. He walked by a door labeled, Captain Raines. He heard loud snoring. *So much for any questions to the Captain.*

He climbed a set of stairs that was missing the second tread from the top, and came out on the top deck. He could see daylight ahead. It was the bridge. There was no one on duty. The Captain's chair had originally been upholstered in blue leather. It now looked like black pieces of shredded leather with cracks and chunks missing.

None of the screens were turn on. Brice heard a clinking sound coming from an open door in the back of the bridge. He walked over and looked in. A middle aged man raised his head from under some large electronic device. "Don't get up seaman." He stared at Brice for a few seconds.

"No seaman. RadCo. Here repair and overhaul radar arrays." Brice knew he was a Spaniard from his accent. The RadCo was most likely a Spanish company too

Brice nodded. "Hello, I'm Lieutenant Brice, the tactical officer. Is the radar the only thing you are here to repair?" The man slipped out from under the massive array of electronic gear. He struggled to stand. He was somewhat over weight. There was a loud rude noise. *He must suffer from an indigestion problem.*

"Jhola, my name Phillip. Si, radar only we service." Brice could barely understand his English.

"How long until the units are operational?"

"Been on job two months. Find problem this week. Both units fried. Have to replace. My boss, he ordered the parts. Will be few weeks. They come China."

Brice was dumbfounded, their top secret surveillance systems were made in China to spy on Chinese ships. What a joke. "Thanks Phillip. I guess I'll be seeing you around for a while yet." He nods, bends over, makes another rude noise and crawls back under the rack of electronics.

Brice left the bridge and went down one deck. He walked as far toward the bow as possible. The large deck gun was fed ammunition from a reinforced circular room below the gun turret. If the room was hit, the exploding ammo would be directed upward. The poor guys operating the gun would be launched into outer space.

Three men in coveralls were struggling to man-handle a large piece of machinery. Brice stood and watched until they finally got it to where they wanted it. They sat down to get their breath. One saw Brice and nudged the others.

"I'm Lieutenant Brice. Who are you?

One of the men stood. In a breathless voice said, "I'm Bob, he pointed at a bald headed man, this is Curley and he is Melvin. We work for NUF, North Umberland Foundry in Wiltshire. We manufacture these baby's. This one is rust-stuck in a 15 degree position to Port and will have to be replaced. We are dismantling it. The new one is due here by the end of November."

Brice was amazed. So far the Radar is from some Chinese company, maintenance by a Spanish company, the cannon is from the UK and he'd not be at all surprised if the engines were not from Detroit.

He walked as far as he could to the stern. A hatch was open to the engine room. Several men were busy doing something to a large machine. One looked up and smiled as he climbed up the ladder and stuck out his hand. "I'm John Brock. We are from Caterpillar in Iowa." *Well that completed the circle, nothing was made in Australia.*

He shook Brock's hand. "I'm Lt. Brice, the tactical officer." He looked at me as if I was some alien that had just stepped off the space ship. He nodded and went down the ladder and resumed his work.

On the way back to the bridge, Brice ran into Seaman McDuffie. "Seaman, who is in charge when the Captain is uh, resting?"

He looked at Brice. "Gonzales was second in command. After he became ill with Covid, no one wanted the job. I guess you are now."

Oh crap. I've never commanded personnel before.

"Where can I get a full roster of the ship's company?

"The Captain, I suppose. We don't have a paymaster. He died eight months ago from Covid also. No one wanted the job after he died."

"Have all the crew been vaccinated?" He looked puzzled.

"Vaccinated?"

Brice was getting a bit panicky. The HMAS Robertson was one step from sinking, the Captain was a drunk, with no one in charge and most of the essential equipment was made in the UK or by the Yanks or the top secret stuff by China and maintained by the Spanish and on top of that the crew has no clue what the pandemic is all about. *This is a disaster.*

He wondered how a ship like this got so far under the fleet radar that if it sank today, it would be years, if ever, before it would be missed.

Chapter Three

Langley, Virginia

Donovan sat at his desk reading a report from an analyst who sat at another desk somewhere in the massive CIA complex. The conclusion was, the AUKUS agreement had not been received well by most who read it. The Chinese were in a tizzy fit, the French weeping to the world how they had been screwed over by the Aussies. No one in the US cared one way or the other. The Aussies were outwardly non-committal and inwardly laughing up their sleeves and the Brits snickered behind closed doors. The Canadians took their normal approach, "What eh?"

Nothing in the report indicated who may have leaked the AUKUS agreement to the press. Donovan suspected the Chinese. They had the most to gain and were pissed at the idea of losing their domination over the Aussies' South Pacific waters. If the Aussies had a nuclear sub, they would be a formidable force to deal with.

Donovan decided he would start with the French and call his opposite in the French DGSI (General Directorate for Internal Security.) He opened his contacts list. He selected one and pressed the call icon.

Somewhere in France

The phone rang three or four times before someone answered. "Bonjour"

"This is Donovan; I need to speak to Kluso."

"No English, s'il te plait"

Donovan made a face and yelled, **"Put someone on that speaks English!"** Silence.

A minute later a sultry female voice asked, "With whom may I have the pleasure of speaking with?" Mike's lips curled into a frown.

"I'm Mike Donovan; I need to speak to Kluso."

"I'm sorry sir; we don't have anyone with that name here."

"What the hell! Who is this?"

"This is Madam Fresco's bordello." Donovan held out the phone and looked at it as if it had a virus crawling out of the ear piece. He had heard that name before, when he was on a case that took him to Paris. He immediately dropped the phone to its base. He opened a desk drawer and took out a can of Lysol and sprayed the phone and immediately deleted the number from his phone's contact list.

Kluso will have to be on his own. The French were wagging a finger at the UK and the Yanks anyway, claiming the Yanks and the Brits conspired to derail the French consortium building the Aussie sub.

CIA Headquarters-Virginia

Col. McClusky, MI-6's super sleuth was brought up to date on the AUKUS agreement by his opposite at the C.I.A, Mike Donovan. It was fairly straight forward. Someone with a top security clearance had copied the entire document and leaked it to the world press. There were three original documents, one in London, one in the Pentagon in Washington, D.C. and one in the Russell Complex in Canberra, Australia.

Donovan and McClusky went back to the days of Desert Storm. Things were much simpler then. It was **them** and **US**. These days, McClusky thought, were so muddled up with politics; it was hard to tell who the good guys were or who the bad guys were. There were more bad guys, so that made it somewhat easier.

Donovan suggested that they meet and come up with a strategy. The meeting would be in Canberra, Australia in two days.

McClusky had Commodore Thomas's office prepare a list of all who had access to the AUKUS document and any surveillance footage of the room where the documents were kept.

Donovan was doing the same with NCIS (Naval Criminal Investigation Service). All surveillance footage from the department of the Navy's top secret records room was copied onto a thumb drive.

NCIS assigned one of their top agents, Tina Rosenberg, to be the Navy's lead investigator.

NCIS had no authority outside the US, but Donovan's contacts were extensive and would close the gap for NCIS. Donovan made a decision to take a back seat and assist Rosenberg. She would be coming along to Canberra for the meeting with McClusky. The CIA was not authorized, technically, to conduct any business within the United States, so NCIS was the agency responsible.

Agent Rosenberg was a tall shapely woman. She had been married to a lawyer, but that ended a couple of years ago. She was dedicated to her job and was the top agent in the Washington NCIS office.

They both arrived on time at Andrews Air Force Base for the flight to Australia with a brief stop in Honolulu. They each carried a laptop. A Corporal took their luggage and disappeared.

The plane was a new Galaxy class and roomy with actual airliner type seats. The flight time from Washington to Canberra was twenty hours, including the stop in Honolulu. Donovan would use most of that time to watch the video recordings collected at the Pentagon.

Rosenberg made herself comfortable and slept most of the way to Honolulu. There were five other non-military passengers. Donovan recognized one of the passengers as a senator from a mid western state.

After several hours of staring at the videos on his laptop, he became tired and decided to take a nap. He slept right through the stopover in Honolulu. When he awoke, three of the other non-military passengers had gotten off in Honolulu. He went back to sleep.

Rosenberg fired up her laptop and began watching the hours of footage they had been given. No one was sure where the leak occurred or why.

Canberra International Airport

The Air Force Galaxy touched down right on time at Fairbairn, the RAAF's VIP airport, part of the Canberra International Airport. The Fairbairn airport was generally used by only high government officials and international government heads.

The Galaxy was a large plane and was required to park some distance from the terminal building. Donovan wondered if they had to walk to the building, it had to be over two kilometers away. As they deplaned, there was a man standing at the bottom of the stairs.

Mr. Donovan and Ms. Rosenberg welcome to Australia, my name is Sergeant Elmer. I'm here to greet you and take you to your hotel. Please follow me. Elmer was dressed in an Australian Royal Air Force dress uniform.

Donovan looked around. There were two Bombardier Challenger 604s parked close to the Fairbairn terminal along with two Bell Six passenger Helicopters. He figured the Challengers were used to shuttle the brass round. A small golf cart like vehicle was parked about ten meters from the stairs leading from the monster plane.

Rosenberg walked briskly with Elmer silently at her side toward the vehicle. She observed the other two passengers walking ahead of her and obviously not being offered any assistance to get to the terminal. One man kept turning and looking back and was obviously interested in her and possibly Donovan. She discreetly removed her iPhone and pretended to take a selfie. She got a great shot of their faces looking directly into the camera. She pressed an icon of an app that would send the photo directly to NCIS for facial recognition.

Donovan grinned at her clandestine picture taking. He wondered who the men were and why she took their picture. It would wait until they were in a less public place to ask.

They had been pre-cleared through customs and immigration. Elmer motioned for them to follow him. He pushed open a door to a private car park area. There was one car, a new Rolls-Royce. The driver jumped out and opened the rear door. He was dressed in a formal chauffeur's uniform. Rosenberg climbed into the roomy back.

"Sergeant Elmer where are our bags. Elmer turned to the driver who nodded toward the back of the car.

"Sir they are in the boot," said Elmer. Donovan was impressed. The baggage got to the car before he did.

"Sergeant Elmer, has Colonel McClusky arrived?"

"No sir, not for another hour or so." I will not be riding with you to the hotel." He handed a card to Mike. "Here is my card. If you need anything, please phone the number at anytime and someone will assist you. Enjoy your stay." He nodded and walked back to the stairs leading up to the enormous plane.

Chapter Four

Aeroport de Paris – Orly

Orly airport is fifteen kilometers south of Paris and was originally an American Air Force Base during the early part of the cold war.

Two men in civilian attire stood in a queue of fifty or more of French military personnel. Francois DePaul who's fake ID was Alfonso Kluso, was not a happy camper. First he was ordered to be accompanied by some political clerk, John Lofgren. He had no idea who or what Lofgren represented or if Lofgren knew Kluso's real name. As soon as he was in a secure area, he would check out Mr. Lofgren.

The office of French Security texted DePaul that this was the only non-commercial flight. It was a direct flight to Toronto, Canada chartered to take a bunch of French military officers for some sort of special training.

From Toronto he and Lofgren were scheduled to board a Royal Canadian Air Force plane. He was not sure where it would connect to for his final destination of Canberra, Australia. DePaul/Kluso thought someone said Tahiti. The estimated total time was an unbelievable fifty three hours.

Kluso dragged his heavy bag along the concourse at Orly. He looked at Lofgren as they stood in the queue. Lofgren looked to be in his mid forties. Clean shaven with blow dried hair. Kluso wondered if he was, uh, different.

"Mr. Kluso, Have you done this before?" asked Lofgren.

DePaul/Kluso seemed shocked at the question. But since he called him by his fake name he felt better.

The guy doesn't know who I am. "No. I always fly commercial, but someone in the Foreign Office thought they could save a little money if we hitched a ride on a military flight."

DePaul didn't have time to confer with the Admiral. He did text the Admiral's office and explained his flight information. He had hoped they would have time to make commercial connections. At least his profile was as low key as it could get. No spy in the east or west would look for Alfonso Kluso on a military flight to hell.

Toronto, Canada

Nine hours later the chartered Air France 757 landed in Toronto. Kluso and Lofgren pulled their bags from the overhead bin and waited in the queue to deplane. There were at least fifty French military officers on the flight. No one paid Lofgren or Kluso any notice. They finally reached the terminal building. A uniformed airline employee was giving instructions as to where Immigration and Customs was located.

Kluso and Lofgren saw the sign and got into another queue. Kluso finally reached the Immigration desk. He handed his special passport with his fake name to the officer, who entered his name and passport number into a computer. The officer seemed surprised and tapped a few keys. He read the screen carefully. "Sir, you are to report to the Air Canada security office after you go through customs. He handed Kluso's passport back. Kluso nodded and pushed his bag on to the next booth.

Lofgren handed his passport to the same officer. "What the Hell? VIP's on a military flight?" The officer sized up Lofgren, stamped his passport and told him to follow his friend through customs.

Their bags were not opened. They exited the customs desk and pulled their bags along to a sign that read, Air Canada Security Office. Kluso pushed the door open to a spacious office with one uniformed security officer sitting behind a glass window. She appeared to be entering data into her computer.

Kluso tapped on the window. She looked up for a second or so and then back to her typing. Lofgren stood patiently behind Kluso who gave the window a second tap. The officer finally opened the window. In a voice that was obviously annoyed, "May I help you?"

"Yes, the immigration officer said to report here." He handed his passport and nodded to Lofgren to do the same. She took the documents and entered the numbers and names into her computer. She stared at the screen for several seconds.

"Mr. Kluso and Mr. Lofgren you are to go to gate 11B. Your plane is waiting for you." She smiled and blushed at Kluso. He smiled back as he took his and Lofgren's passports from her offered hand.

"How far is gate 11B?"

"Sir I will have a cart take you. Please stand over by the door. They will be here in two minutes."

"Thank you." Kluso dragged his bag to the door. Lofgren was right behind. The door popped open almost as soon as they reached it. An elderly man in a uniform that had seen its better days did a shallow bow and grabbed Kluso's bag. The bag must have weighed as much as he did.

"Uh, thank you, but I can handle my bag," said Kluso. The poor man looked relieved not to have to pick up the bag. A large passenger golf cart was parked on the other side of the door.

Kluso placed his bag in the baggage area and motioned for Lofgren to do the same. They climbed into the cart and the elderly man got behind the wheel. He reached into a breast pocket and put on a pair of glasses that appeared to be a centimeter thick.

Kluso looked at Lofgren who had a horror stricken look on his face as if he was to board the world's highest roller coaster. It took a good ten minutes to reach gate 11B. There were some close calls, but no one was run over.

Kluso and Lofgren pulled their bags off the cart. The old man did not wait around for a tip, he immediately left. There was one person behind the counter at 11B. No one was seated in the waiting area.

Kluso thought everyone had boarded and they were holding the flight for them to board. Kluso walked up to the counter. The man looked up.

"I'm Kluso and this is Lofgren. We were told to come here for our flight." The man snapped to attention and put the comic book away he had been reading.

"Sir, I need your passports." They handed over their passports. He entered them into his computer. He pressed a key or two and the printer spat out two boarding passes.

Kluso looked at the plane parked at 11B. It was an Air Canada Boeing 777. The man placed the passports and boarding passes on the counter top.

"How long before we can board?"

"Sir, you may board any time you are ready to leave." Kluso looked at the man.

"We are ready now. What time is the flight scheduled to leave?

"Sir, you are the only two passengers. We will leave when you are ready." Kluso looked at Lofgren and shrugged his shoulders. *The Admiral must have gotten my text and made a few changes.*

"Well let's go then." The man nodded and entered a code to open the door to the jet bridge leading to the plane.

"You may leave your luggage here; we will load it for you. Have a comfortable flight." Kluso led the way down the sloping corridor.

Nigel McClusky, MI-6's celebrated secret agent, sat across the concourse at terminal 12B and observed it all. He snapped two pictures with his phone and waited until they were on the jet bridge. He spoke into his iPhone. So far his informant had been dead on. Kluso and some unknown had boarded an Air Canada flight. Kluso could not find any listed flights at gate 11B. He concluded it must be a charter.

Kluso and Lofgren reached the 777's door. Two Air Canada flight attendants stood at attention as they approached. "Sirs, you may pick any seat you want, you are our only passengers. As soon as you are settled in your seats, I will serve you a cocktail. Dinner will be served in one hour. Welcome aboard Air Canada."

"Uh, what is our destination?" Kluso had a worried look. *Was this some sort of kidnapping scheme?*

The flight attendant looked confused. "Sir, we were charted to go directly to Canberra, Australia."

"Thank you. Fix me a double single malt Scotch."

McClusky pocketed his iPhone as he watched Kluso disappear down the jet bridge. He walked down the concourse to gate 9A. There was no one in the gate area. He walked to the jet bridge door and entered a code. The door clicked open and McClusky walked through.

Chapter Five

Eleven Thousand Meters

The British government's Grumman II leveled off at eleven thousand meters. The quiet hum of its engines was soothing. Nigel McClusky sat back in his leather seat and enjoyed his diet coke listening to those four Rolls-Royce engines pushing him over the North Pole and to the Pacific Ocean.

We Brits know how to treat our secret agents. The Foreign office gave McClusky a fake name, Richard Jenkins. He was posing as a wealthy business man on his way to purchase a French software company in Australia.

He didn't know anything about software, but that was not necessary. His controller told him someone was to meet him and do all the technical stuff.

His mission was to find out what the 'Frogs' were up to. The rumor among the spy world was that the French were determined to derail the Aussies' new submarine program with the help of the Chinese MSS.

He thought the French went a bit over the top by chartering a Boeing 777 for two people. Kluso was a slippery character. He didn't know who the other guy was, but he uploaded the photos and if he's in the system, he would know before he landed in Canberra.

The flight attendant offered him another diet coke. She smiled and returned to the rear of the business jet. The flight was thirteen hours from Toronto to Canberra over the pole. He knew that half the world's spies would be falling all over themselves to find out what was happening. As far as he knew, the Yanks and the Brits were in the driver's seat. At least he hoped so.

Canberra International Airport

The business jet taxied to the business terminal. There were four other business jets parked at jet bridges. McClusky didn't recognize any of the planes. They had no markings, and neither did his.

The door was opened by the copilot and McClusky made his way to the terminal. There were two Aussie officers at the combo immigration and customs desk. He offered his fake passport and declaration form. They did not open his one bag. The female officer looked at his picture on the passport and looked up at him. She smiled, stamped an empty page.

He looked out on the vast tarmac and saw the huge Yank plane in the distance. Loud engine noise came from the tarmac as an Air Canada Boeing 777 taxied to the air bridge of a commercial airline gate. He saw the gate number was 5A. He looked at the female officer. "It must be show time. Who's got the biggest?" She did not smile.

He picked up his passport and bag and headed to the concourse. He made it to gate 5A just as Kluso and the unknown man made it to the customs and Immigration line. He stood back and watched. He looked at his iPhone hoping the unidentified man had been named. Nothing had turned up yet.

A shapely young woman walked up behind him and tapped him on the shoulder. He nearly wet himself.

"Hello Mr. Jenkins. I'm Louise Mathurne. I'm your aide and guide."

"Hello. I thought we were to meet at the hotel, but thanks for meeting me here. Are we far from the hotel?"

"No sir. It is only five minutes to the hotel. I have a car waiting." McClusky looked back to where Kluso and the unknown man had been standing in the queue. They were gone, Bummer.

"I have only this carry on so I'm ready to go." She smiled and offered to help with his only bag. He shook his head and put the strap over his shoulder and motioned for her to lead the way.

They began walking toward the door marked Transportation. McClusky looked around hoping to spot Kluso. Kluso and unknown were gone.

They exited the terminal and she walked to a four door Rover parked with a driver behind the wheel. She opened the back door and motioned for him to climb in with his bag. She took a seat in the front beside the driver and they were on their way to the hotel Realm.

Chapter Six

Hotel Realm

The Rover pulled into the sweeping drive leading to the front of the hotel. A uniformed attendant opened the back door. McClusky/Jenkins emerged with his backpack. Louise Mathurne was already headed to the front desk. It was obvious that this was not her first time as an aide to a rich and important person.

McClusky/Jenkins followed her into the massive lobby. This was certainly for the rich and famous. Everything in the lobby spoke of money. The chairs were exquisite leather; the paintings on the walls were original masterpieces.

He saw Mathurne at the front desk talking to one of the clerks as he moved quietly behind her. She received two key cards and turned to find McClusky right behind her.

"Sir, I will take you to your suite. Unless you want to rest, we can begin outlining our strategy. The suite has two bedrooms and a working office. I think you will be well pleased. She smiled and headed to the bank of lifts.

There were only four suites on the top floor. She passed the key card over the sensor. The door clicked and she pushed it open.

McClusky was not expecting such a large suite. It had to be at least 200 square meters. His home was not this large. There were two doors leading off the sitting room on either side. One was a super bedroom with a large attached office containing every amenity from a computer to high speed copier/printer and the other door led to a king size bedroom.

Mathurne watched McClusky/Jenkins look carefully at the suite. She was worried he would not approve. "Sir is all to your liking?"

He had to get into his role as mister rich man. "Yes this will do. My business will only take a few days. He smiled at her."

She smiled back and went to the bedroom and checked all. Satisfied, she returned to the huge sitting room. Is there anything I can do for you until our business meeting?

"Ms. Mathurne, thank you."

"Please call me Louise."

"Louise, it is early in the afternoon. I need to rest for an hour or so and then I would like to meet with you to discuss the acquisition."

"Yes sir. I will be here at 4pm."

"That's perfect." He walked to the door and held it for her to leave. She brushed lightly against him as she departed. He smiled.

Chapter Seven

Spy

Yen Lee had been embedded in the secret Boat Works in Adelaide for ten months. His unique experience in welding had assured him a job. He was assigned to a team headed by a French master welder.

At first the French boss watched everything Lee did. Then after two months, the French boss disappeared from the job site. A British man took over and began to make major changes in the assignments.

Reporting

The boat yard was closed on Sunday. Lee stayed as inconspicuous as possible. There were several other Chinese working at the boat works. He avoided them as much as possible. His MSS contact had assured Lee it was a mission that would give him great rewards and he would move quickly to MSS Officer Rank. Yen Lee's mission was to report the progress of the sub's building to his handler in Beijing each Sunday morning at 10am Beijing time.

Yen Lee got up early Sunday morning. The new Brit boss had changed the way things were done. The ship yard now worked on Sundays. All workers were scheduled every other Sunday with overtime pay.

The pay was twenty times what he would make in China. He could now afford a nice apartment and even purchased a motorcycle. It was used, but better than anything he could buy in China. He thought he just might stay in Australia.

He turned on his laptop and began typing a coded message that he would post on his fake FaceBook page.

Lee nibbled on a piece of toast as he scrolled down the page. He knew something was happening at the top level of the boat yard. Three Brits and Three Yanks were the new bosses. They were fair and seemed to have loads of experience in building Subs. No word given as to what happened to the French bosses.

A large building constructed on the water front was known as N-5 and was off limits to all but a handpicked group. His new boss told him on Friday he would be transferred to building N-5 on Monday. No one knew what was being built in building N-5. He finished the coded message and posted it on his FaceBook page. He waited for a *like* to indicate his handler received the message.

A reply came back. ***Get pictures of the family***. This was unusual. The reply ordered him to get pictures of the object in building N-5. He clicked *like* to tell his handler he had received and understood the message.

Detection

On the floor above Lee's apartment, two people sat opposite each other staring at images on their laptops. The female smiled. I got him. He just got a message posted on FaceBook. I copied the message. The male sitting across from her tapped a few keys. "I just uploaded the session to Canberra. You were right about Lee, he is MSS. How did you sort him out so quickly?"

"I followed the money. He has not sent one dollar to China, most unusual. The address he gave in Hong Kong is a fake. He checked out too clean. Most of the other Asians working on the project have a police trail of miss deeds. Lee is squeaky clean and he has only one friend on FB. The one he just got a message from is most likely his handler. Canberra will be able to trace the IP address. It seems he is to get pictures of the project. We should be able to arrest him in the act."

The Secret Project

Monday was a dull rainy day. Lee put on his rain gear and rode his motorcycle through the light rain to the ship yard. He parked in his usual space, took out the rain cover from the saddle bags and covered the bike. He entered building N-5. Four armed Marines stood inside the entrance. One asked for his ID. Yen Lee wore his ID on a lanyard around his neck. He removed the badge and handed it to the Marine seated at a table with a computer. The soldier entered Lee's employee ID and snapped a picture of him. The Marine handed the ID back and told him to follow the blue line on the floor.

The blue line disappeared below a huge steel door. Lee approached the door. It opened automatically. As soon as he stepped through the door, it banged loudly as it closed behind him and another door opened further down the short hallway. He carefully walked through the second door. His boss was seated at a desk. He looked up at Yen Lee and smiled. "Welcome to Building N-5. You will be issued new work clothes. There is a room with a locker with your name down that hall. You are to leave all personal items including cell phones and any other electronic devices in the locker. Len Lee nodded and walked to the end of the hall. A door labeled Locker Room was open.

Several men were in various stages of changing their clothes. No one spoke. Lee walked down the long row of metal lockers until he saw his name. He opened the locker door. Inside was a pair of coveralls with his name sewn above the left pocket. On the shelf he saw a towel and a bar of soap in a wicker basket. He chose a bench in front of his locker and sat.

Lee looked around. No one was paying any attention to him. He sat on the bench and removed his shoes. He removed his rain gear and hung it on hooks inside the locker. He emptied his pockets and placed his cell phone, a few coins and wallet in a small wicker basket on the shelf. He had nothing else in his pockets. He removed all of his outer clothing, hung them carefully on the hooks and put on the royal blue coveralls. A perfect fit. He carefully put his shoes back on and closed his locker and wondered what he was to do next. He sat back down on the bench. Several other workers had done the same. Several minutes went by. He noticed a camera in the ceiling.

After about five minutes his boss came through the door. He held an iPad and read a list of names. As he read the names each person raised his hand. Yen Lee raised his hand when his name was read. Two of the workers were from his previous team. They turned and nodded when they heard his name.

"Men, you have been selected to work on a new project. It is top secret. That means you each must sign this secrets act document and you will not speak of what you see or do in this building. That means families, friends and even your work mates. If you have a question about what you are working on you ask me and no one else. Form a queue and sign the document. Afterwards wait in the hallway."

First view of the Project

Yen Lee signed the document and stood in the hall with the other men. There were twenty-six. The British boss came out, "Men follow me." He removed a card from his pocket and waved it over a sensor on a door next to the locker room. They all filed into the new facilities. It was enormous. The large skeleton of the sub they had worked on for eight months had been moved to this building on a huge rail carriage. The sub stretched from one end of the dry dock to the far back wall. There was a crew working on something next to the superstructure. The sub looked like a large fish with its bones exposed.

Lee saw several other teams standing and listening as their bosses explained something. They were too far away to hear the words distinctly.

Assignments

Lee's boss called all his team to huddle around. "Men, the French company is no longer building the sub. A consortium of the UK and the US has taken over the project. The sub is now going to be a nuclear machine. All of this of course is top secret. You each signed a document that makes it a capital crime to speak about your job and of course any details concerning the sub." He waited for all of that to settle in. "Your job is to assemble the 'hot box' that will contain the nuclear engine. It will be very exacting work and will require top skills. You are that team. I have observed each of you and your skills meet all of my requirements."

He opened a briefcase and removed a stack of papers. "These are your assignments. I will give one to each team. Read over the specifications and measurements. Be careful to select only the specified materials. You will work with a partner. Each pair will take turns inspecting the other's work. There is no room for any short cuts or sub-standard work. There will be a fifteen percent increase in your pay. Your future with this project depends on your ability to do your best work. There will be no questions. I will speak to each of you individually and will answer any questions at that time. You may pick your work mate and if you don't have a preference, I will appoint someone to be with you. Those who know their preference please move over to the platform and wait." There were six men with no work mates. The boss quickly selected and paired up the three remaining teams. He began to pass out the job assignments.

Work Team

Lee was paired up with a man from Hughenden, Queensland. He had seen the man before working on the sub. The boss handed Lee one of the assignment papers.

Lee introduced himself to his work mate and the man said his name was Archer. They nodded at each other and joined all the teams standing on the platform that connected to the new sub.

The document showed the exact location of their assignment. Each of the work areas had an alphabetic letter painted on the hull. Theirs was M.

The boss told them to go to their work areas and become familiar with what they were to accomplish. Lee handed the paper to Archer who read it carefully and pointed to their area. They headed to the 'M' site. It was a bare space with the superstructure only partially constructed. The assignment was to complete the outer hull and the supporting structure for the inter-hull and 'Hot Box'. The materials for the job were already on the scaffold.

"Well it looks simple enough. The crane is in position to hoist the plates into position and we weld the units to the superstructure," said Archer. Lee nodded he concurred.

The crane's operator was not part of their group. The skill required to operate the crane was totally different from those skills the teams brought to the project.

Instructions

Lee saw the boss heading toward his area. "Lee and Archer, you are to use this mobile to communicate with the crane operator." He handed Lee the phone. "When you are ready for the plates to be put into place, press the call button to alert the operator that you need to speak to him. Give him your location letter and what you want moved. Spray your letter on the plate to be moved." He handed Archer a can of orange spray paint. "Any questions?"

"Sir, where are the facilities?"

The boss smiled. "I was wondering who would ask that question." He pointed to a large blue door across the platform. "That leads to the facilities.

You must both go to the area together. There is an area for waiting for your mate. Remember there is to be no conversations with anyone about where you work or what you are working on. Each team must maintain total secrecy about their assignments."

Lee nodded and looked at Archer. "Sir, where are our tools, masks and gloves?" asked Lee.

"Your tools will be brought here by a supply team. The welding helmet and gloves are in your lockers. We will begin at 0700 tomorrow. You will be returning to the locker room shortly and you may have the remainder of the day off. Wait for the whistle to blast three times indicating the end of your shift. Then go to the locker room."

Both men looked at each other and smiled. It was the first time they had paid time off. The boss moved on to another team.

It was only ten minutes until the whistle blasted three times. All the teams headed for the exit to the locker room. Yen Lee and Archer walked side by side. Neither spoke.

When they reached the locker room, each team began to put on their street clothes. Lee checked his locker. A new welding helmet and gloves were on the shelf on top of the wicker basket. He tried on the helmet. It fit snugly and the view plate was clear. That was different.

Archer observed him. "The plate turns dark when you strike an arc. It is sensitive to ultraviolet light." Lee nodded. Great, that was one of the annoying things about welding, pulling your helmet up and down to view your work.

Lee carefully removed his shoes. He had not had an opportunity to take any pictures today. Maybe tomorrow he would have more time.

The two observers watched Lee on the job site. The newly installed cameras were High Definition and the view could be controlled with a joy stick, it was perfect. The observation was auto recorded onto a computer. They saw nothing that would indicate Lee had taken any pictures.

Chapter Eight

Yulin Sub Base

Chi Lu Chong arrived for duty at the Yulin sub base private airport. Chong walked down the jet bridge and looked around. He was not sure where to go.

A young seaman held a small sign with his name on it and escorted him to the base. They entered a lift that took them down many underground floors. They emerged into a small ante room. His escort told him to have a seat and wait until someone came to escort him the remainder of the way. He told Chong to leave his baggage. A porter would take it to his sub. The escort promptly saluted and left.

Chong waited nearly half an hour before anyone came. He was totally unaware he had been under surveillance the entire time. A man in a lab coat escorted him to a room where he was photographed, peered into a machine to record his retina, finger printed, DNA swabbed and blood sample taken. He was then led to another room with a table and two chairs. It was obviously an interrogation room. The man pointed at a chair and left the room.

A middle age woman came in about ten minutes later wearing a white lab coat. She introduced herself as Dr. Wong. She sat down. "Is there anything I can get you, water, food or soft drink?"

Chong shook his head no. She opened a folder that contained no more than two or three sheets of paper. "Where were you born?"

"Hohhot, Inter Mongolia." She looked down at the folder.

"Is your family Han and where did you go to school?"

"Yes my family is third generation Han. I attended Mongolian University. I received my Masters at the University of Beijing."

"What are you assigned to do?"

Chong looked into her eyes. He remembered his handler saying not to talk to anyone about his specialties and assignment. "I'm not authorized to speak about my assignment or my specialty."

She smiled. "Yes, well thank you. You will be escorted to your sub and meet with the Captain."

She left the room. Immediately the door reopened and a uniformed junior officer came in. An electric cart waited in the wide hallway. They boarded the cart. The cart moved quickly down the wide passageway which had a white line painted down the middle, just like a highway.

Ten minutes later the cart entered a huge domed area. There were rows of piers like fingers reaching out into a wide body of water all under roof. Chong counted eleven subs of various sizes tied up to the piers. Workers were moving carts piled with supplies to open hatches on the decks of the subs.

His cart stopped at a sub tied up several piers away from the other boats.

An officer stood at the pier and smiled as Chong got out of the cart. He was expected.

Chapter Nine

Company Purchase

McClusky took a nap and was awakened by a loud buzzing sound coming from the door. He got up, looked at the clock. Local time was 1600. *Crap, meeting time.*

He opened the door and sure enough there stood Louise. She was beaming from ear to ear. "Am I early?"

"No, I forgot the local time and overslept. Come in." She entered and went straight to the office. "I'll be with you in a moment. Make yourself at home." He went to his room and brushed his teeth and combed his hair and joined her in the office.

She had papers spread out on the desk. He sat down. "Bring me into focus on what you have here."

"Sir, I have an offer ready for your signature. I will go over the document. The chairman of the board has a preliminary copy. They are ready to move forward as soon as you agree with the terms."

"I see. Well let's get on with it."

"First, the overall price in Australian Dollars is thirty six million which includes eighteen million in debt. Is that amount correct?"

McClusky was not sure what to do. This deal was jacked up for his cover to find out the French's reaction to AUKUS. The software company's largest client was the Navy. The software company was all French owned and staffed mostly by Australians.

McClusky looked a few seconds at the floor. "For now the price is acceptable, but let's move on to the details. I will have to speak to my legal department before I can finalize the acquisition." She smiled at him and nodded.

"Article one. All software code and plans for updates and new products are to be included in the list of assets. Current market value based on customer's purchases is eleven million. The lease on office space is also an asset. Since they took the lease, the price of comparable space has gone up Twenty five percent in their building. The lease is valued at .25 million.

"Article two. The five company cars are also listed along with one Grumman II, a four year old business jet. They are valued at eighteen million. The amount owed to the lending institution is eighteen million. You would be taking on the debt but no cash outlay." She looked at McClusky. He smiled.

"Article three. There are two hundred computers and various office furniture listed with a market value of one point two million. There is goodwill valued at five million.

Article four. "Staff severance allowance is .55 million." She looked up.

"Why am I paying half a million for severance pay? That's the old company's responsibility."

"Sir, the severance pay is for one person, the chairman. All the other Staff are remaining with the company."

"Hum, I don't like that. I'm taking on eighteen million in debt for cars and an airplane. They should be lucky to find someone to take on this much debt. Do you have a spread sheet with anticipated revenue and expenses for the next three years?"

Louise keyed in some information on her laptop. "Sir, the projected revenue for the next three years comes to thirty million, all under contract to the Australian Navy. The current overhead is five million per year which includes payments for cars and the business jet. If the revenue and expenses can be maintained, the net profit for the three year period is fifteen million. This does not take into consideration any new products being introduced.

McClusky sat thinking. *Damn, I'm in the wrong business.* "Thank you for all the work you have put into this. I'm going to remove the five hundred thousand for the chairman's severance pay and if the deal goes through, I'm giving you that amount." She sat looking at McClusky like he was Father Christmas.

She got up and went around the desk and kissed him. He responded enthusiastically. She sat in his lap and made him feel like he was twenty one again. After several minutes, she kissed him again and got up and took his hand and led him to his bedroom. McClusky giggled all the way.

Chapter Ten

Omni Hotel

Mike Donovan and Tina Rosenberg made it through customs and made their way to the hotel's courtesy van location. Mike had made advance reservations to be taken to the hotel in the hotel's van.

They checked into their rooms and each took a three hour nap. Donovan called McClusky on his cell phone as soon as he awoke. McClusky answered in a breathless voice. Mike thought maybe he had been working out. "McClusky, do you want to have dinner and talk about our plans?"

"Hi Mike, I've got plans for this evening, but breakfast would work for me."

"Okay, we're staying at the Omni near the airport. How about meeting here at 0900 in the coffee shop," said Donovan.

"Sounds great, I'll see you at 0900." He broke the connection and turned back to a smiling Louise. "A business appointment I booked for tomorrow. Now where were we?"

Mike smiled as he pressed the red button to terminate the call. *McClusky doesn't waste time.*

Mike took a shower and put on fresh clothes. He had just poured himself a drink when his phone chirped. "Mike speaking."

"Mike would you like to meet in the bar for a drink?" asked Tina Rosenberg.

"I've got a better idea, how about coming over here and I'll fix you a free drink."

"Good, I'll be right over." Her room was across the hall.

Mike got up and opened the door just as she arrived. "Did you have a nap?"Asked Mike.

"Sort of, I'm not good at these time changes. It took me forever to fall asleep and then I tossed and turned, not very restful."

"What would you like? I've got Scotch, Bourbon and Vodka."

"I'll have Vodka on the rocks with a splash of tonic."

"Coming right up." Mike took a bottle of Vodka from the mini bar and mixed the drink.

Tina reached for the glass and took a long pull. "Have you come to any conclusions on the mystery person that leaked the document?" asked Tina.

"Not really. I watched the video and it was not much help. No one even went near the cabinet containing the document. It may have not been from our side of the pond. I have booked us a breakfast with McClusky. He may have some clues. The Brits are very secretive with their information. They play it very close to the chest, especially if it points to one of their own."

"I watched most of the video on the plane. I concur; no one even opened the cabinet. That leaves the Australians or the British. Who do we talk to on the Aussie team?" asked Tina.

"I placed a call to their investigative branch, the ASIO before we left and have not heard back.

Donovan looked at his watch. "It's 0200 in Washington. They may have notified Langley and because of the time difference, the info hasn't caught up with us yet."

Tina looked puzzled. "You mean the CIA works banker hours. NCIS never shuts down. Someone is on duty 24/7."

"We do have a team on duty 24/7. They route the messages. If it involves an open investigation it goes to the section chief regardless of the time and he calls the necessary parties." He took a sip of his Scotch. His phone chirped.

"This is Mike." He listened and grabbed a pencil and wrote something on a serviette. "Thanks, I will call tomorrow and book an appointment." He broke the connection and looked at his note. "Well, it seems the Aussies want to meet and go over the data. They have assigned an agent to work with us. His name is Mason Livingston."

Omni Hotel Coffee Shop

At 0900, Tina and Mike arrived at the Omni Hotel Coffee Shop. McClusky was seated at a table and motioned for Tina and Mike to join him. "Good morning. I don't think we've met." He held his hand for a handshake.

"Oh sorry, this is Tina Rosenberg of NCIS. She has point on this case."

McClusky gave her a long stare. "My pleasure, I don't think I've worked with the NCIS before. I do know of the good work you do for your Navy."

Tina smiled. "Thank you sir, as you know, NCIS has no jurisdiction outside the US. Mike has been kind enough to join me and take the lead on foreign soil."

McClusky nodded and motioned for all to be seated. "I haven't ordered yet. Let's order and then get down to business." They each picked up a menu and made their selections. The waiter took their orders, poured coffee and disappeared to the kitchen.

"Mike and I have viewed the video of the file room in the Pentagon. We have come to the conclusion no one even went into the cabinet containing the document. That leaves us with Australia and UK," said Tina.

McClusky put his cup down. "Tina, we can't rule out someone may have copied the document before it was placed in the secret archives. I have also viewed the video of our document room. I came to the same conclusion as you. No one entered the security room area where the document was stored during the months after the document was placed in archives. And as I said this does not rule out someone making a copy before it was stored."

Breakfast arrived and they dug in. Mike observed McClusky closely. He seemed more animated than Mike remembered. Something was affecting him and he seemed very relaxed with whatever it was.

Mike looked at McClusky. "Do you have any contacts within the ASIO?" McClusky put his fork down.

"I haven't worked with them in years. All of my contacts have either died or retired."

"I have spoken with the Director-General. He has assigned me an agent. His name is Mason Livingston. I'm to call him this afternoon for a meeting," said Mike. McClusky raised an eyebrow.

"Are you aware one of the French agents, Inspector Kluso and an unknown are here in Canberra?"

It was Donovan's time to be surprised. "No. I thought they had been dismissed and were no longer interested."

"It seems they are very interested. I don't know the fellow that is traveling with Kluso, but I should have his ID later today."

They traded theories back and forth but nothing useful was discussed. They agreed to meet for dinner in the evening at the Omni.

ASIO Headquarters

Mike and Tina sat on hard chairs in a room that was very plain and obviously not meant to impress. A tall man came through the only door opening from the interior. "My name is Arthur Metcalf. Please follow me." He turned and opened the door with a key card and held the door for Tina and Mike to enter.

Mr. Metcalf led them down a carpeted hallway to a suite of offices. There were no names on the doors. Metcalf used his keycard to open one of the many doors. He preceded them into a very large and comfortable looking office. "Please have a seat. The Director-General will be along shortly." He turned and left. Tina was sizing up the office. She saw three different cameras with most likely listening microphones also. She and Mike did not speak. Mike took out his phone and brought up an app that zeroed in on the cameras. He leaned over and showed Tina. She nodded.

A door opened behind a huge desk. A middle aged man came in and sat behind the desk. "My name is Mason Livingston. Our Director-General has asked me to work with you and attempt to analyze why the AUKUS document was leaked to the press. We are at a loss. Who gains, who loses and who are the players."

"Mr. Livingston, we have the same questions. From our perspective, we can't come up with why and at this particular time eight months after it was drafted. We have almost eliminated anyone in the US or UK from getting a copy from the secure documents archive. We have scrubbed the videos and no one even went close to our cabinet containing the document. That does not eliminate the odd chance someone copied the document before it was placed in archive, but why?"

Livingston sat staring at the desktop. "We have another problem you may not be aware of. The Chinese have stepped up their presence in our waters. They also have sent agents to infiltrate the assembly area of the sub.

"With the Covid outbreak, our ships are not fully staffed. We have filled some of the gaps with on shore personnel. Needless to say, this is not ideal. We are stepping up our surveillance of their ships and subs and have dispatched a watcher team to Adelaide."

Tina placed her hand on the desk top "Mr. Livingston, how secure is the assembly facility?"

He looked at her a long time. "We have moved the actual construction of the sub to a class-A facility with the best security system we have. Each employee has been vetted and must go through a procedure before entering the actual construction site. I would be glad to go through all of our protocols."

"I'm sure you have an air tight situation. We are here to help you. We will share anything we find and hope you do the same. The US has a vested interest in making sure nothing goes wrong with the project."

"Yes, well we have uncovered one possible operative. He is Chinese and poses as a welder. We only found out his existence yesterday. Before we take action, we want to observe him. We have means to monitor his connection to his handler. As soon as we have more data on his mission I will inform you. Unless you have anything to report, that is all for today. It is too early to start rounding up the usual." Livingston stood signaling the end of the meeting. He shook hands with both Tina and Mike. He pressed a button on his desk and the door opened with Metcalf standing at attention.

"Please follow me." They left the office area and were back at the front waiting room. "Would you like for me to fetch a taxi for you?"

Mike smiled and said, "No thank you. We can take it from here." Livingston did a shallow bow and closed the large metal door.

Tina saw a taxi rank a few meters down from the front entrance. She nudged Mike and they walked to a waiting taxi. Mike told the driver to take them to the Omni Hotel. Other than directions, Mike and Tina did not speak again until they exited the taxi at the door of their hotel. He surmised the driver was an employee of the ASIO and the taxi was wired to record video and audio of passengers. At least that is what the CIA would do.

Chapter Eleven

Fu Win Signature

The Fu Win was a super secret nuclear sub in the Chinese Navy. The sleek sub eased out of the pen and headed to open sea.

A fishing boat with two fishermen were throwing their net when a chime sounded below their deck. One of the fishermen went below and pressed a button. A computer screen told them a sub by the name Fu Win was leaving the base. The device recorded the signature of the sub as it left for open water. The fisherman pressed the transmit key and a burst transmission beamed to a satellite high above, completely undetected. A Chinese patrol boat cruised nearby. The fishermen were regularly spotted in the area and ignored.

Tour of the Fu Win

Chong had only seen the control room and his cabin. He was told there were several areas of the sub off limits. He sat on his bunk in his cabin. It was larger than he had imagined.

The door buzzer sounded. He opened the door and the Captain stood smiling at him. "Sir, please come in." Chong opened a compartment in the wall and lowered a seat. The Captain nodded and sat down.

"Chong, you were highly recommended by your professors at the Beijing University. We are tasked with experimenting with some very secret equipment. You are to evaluate the effectiveness of the devices and report to your superior. I am not your superior, but only your host. This mission is all about you." Chong looked dumbfounded.

"Sir, no one told me anything about what I was to do. What devices am I to evaluate?"

"I'm not sure what they are called, but one is to measure radiation created by a nuclear powered ship, the other is a long range listening device to detect engine noise from ships. There is a third device, but I was told nothing about its purpose. I guess your superior will explain what it is for." The Captain stared at Chong for a full minute. "I will take you to the areas where the devices are installed. It is off limits to all but you and of course me and my number one. So, if you are ready, we can get that part of my assignment completed." The Captain got up and waited until Chong opened the door. They left the officer's area of the sub and headed toward the bow.

Radiation Detection System

The Captain told Chong to use his ID badge and to place it over the scanner beside the door. The door clicked open. He told Chong to enter. The Captain remained in the hall.

Chong looked at the equipment. The monitors were active and showed charts and graphs. It was similar to the test equipment he had used in the University lab. There was a bound manual on the desk. The machine had four monitors and a keyboard with a joystick. He had used the same equipment at the lab to detect micro emissions of nuclear radiation.

On the left was a door to another room. The room was much larger than the current room. Chong entered the room. There were four monitors, keyboard and two joysticks. The equipment was not active. The control panel was left of the main console. Chong noticed an ordinary key stuck out from the panel that was required to turn on the equipment. The manual was open to the first page. He read the title. It was in English. He stepped back to the small first room. "Captain why distribute the equipment to two rooms?"

"Mr. Chong, this room is too small to accommodate all the equipment, so they used the adjacent room for the overflow. Is that going to be a problem?"

"No sir." Chong went back to the larger room and picked up the manual.

TOP SECRET

Ultra long range sonar receptor

Chong leafed through a few pages of the manual, all English. He was fluent in English and had no problem with the manual. He looked at the control panel. All of the controls were in English. He had not looked at the manual in the previous room, and wondered if all manuals were in English. He would check this out later.

Chong stepped back into the hall and pulled the door shut behind him. The Captain nodded and led the way further down the hallway. This time they traveled to the very end of the hall. There were torpedoes in racks along both sides of the hallway.

Special Room

This door was different. The door had an eye scanner and a card reader.

"Mr. Chong, I'm not allowed in this room. It is for your eyes only. You must look into the eye scanner and then put your ID card over the scanner."

Chong looked at the eye scanner and pressed his right eye over the lens. He heard a mechanical click and a green light came on. It was blinking. He placed his ID badge over the scanner. The green light stayed steady and the door clicked open. The Captain backed away from the door and stood several paces down the hallway.

Chong entered the room. He was impressed. The room contained a desk, a rack containing a large transceiver with other electronic gear.

A small monitor showed the ship's location in longitude and latitude. A manual was on the desk opened to the first page. Again it was in English. He examined the manual. The equipment was to be used at precisely 1700 Beijing time each day. The clock on the wall was on Beijing time. He had three hours before he was to use the comms equipment.

Chong stepped out into the hallway and pulled the door closed behind him. The light over the eye scanner turned red. There was a pronounced click as the door locked.

"Sir, I'm not sure what I am to do, but I assume the manuals will tell me. Why are they in English?"

"The crew that installed this equipment was not forthcoming into what was the purpose, but referred me to the agent in charge. I never saw an agent. I'm guessing about why the manuals are in English. No one on board can read or speak English but you. So, you are on your own. The door to the first room has been programmed to only admit you, me and my executive officer, with the exception of this room, it is only for you."

Chong nodded he understood. "Sir, I would like to tour the remainder of the boat so I know where the mess hall is located." The Captain smiled.

They went up stairs to another corridor. This one was short an ended into the sub's control room. There were at least a dozen men and one woman at various stations. He noticed the depth was fifty meters, speed forty five knots. The Captain allowed him a few minutes to observe before moving out of the control room to another set of stairs. These ended at a long corridor. There were some open areas without doors. The mess hall was one, an entertainment room and a gym. Chong was impressed.

The Captain opened another door with a set of stairs leading down. The generation room was an open area. The generators were huge. The reactor room was not open. The lead lined room was sealed and was to be opened only by qualified crew.

The Captain explained most of the functions the men were performing at seated stations around the large area.

"Sir, thank you for the personal tour, I must return to my area to prepare for my first report."

The Captain nodded and walked away and up the stairs. Chong remained for several minutes observing the men controlling the various engine functions. He left and climbed the stairs. He saw the corridor continued around the sub's control room. He would not have to pass through the control room to get to the special rooms.

First Report

Chong passed his cabin and proceeded to the end of the hallway. He placed his eye on the scanner and placed his ID card over the sensor. The door clicked open.

He took a seat in front of the rack. There was a camera mounted on top of the monitor. So, he was to be observed while in this room. So be it. He opened the manual. All the instructions referred to the equipment as comms. The second page indicated how to use the controls. Simple, engage the on switch, wait thirty seconds. Press the transmit button and wait for a connection. That was it, no hunting for a frequency was necessary.

Everything was controlled by a computer also in the rack of equipment and was active. On the third page was a critical instruction.

Notify the captain to bring the boat to antenna depth and deploy the high gain antenna five minutes before transmitting. Chong noticed for the first time, a phone handset hanging in a recess on the rack. He picked up the handset. Immediately, a voice announced he had connected to the control room.

"This is Science Officer Chong. Please connect me with the Captain."

"Yes sir, please hold."

Several seconds later, "This is the Captain. Mr. Chong what can I do for you?"

"Sir, my instructions state at 1700 Beijing time you are to bring the sub to high gain antenna depth and deploy the antenna."

"Thank you for the reminder. I was given orders to do that every day while you are on board. I will call you on this phone as soon as the antenna is deployed."

"Sir, thank you. We have plenty of time. I will be here at 1700, Chong out." He replaced the handset. Chong opened the room with the sonar receiver. He read most of the manual. Nothing was different from the lab equipment he had used in school. He went into the radiation detection room.

The manual was short. He would use the joy stick to aim something outside the sub. The device would detect very small amounts of radiation that escaped a nuclear reactor. There is a distinct marker for the radiation spectrum from Plutonium than from other heavy metals. Any leakage from this sub would not show because the marker was altered to be undetected by the equipment.

There was no doubt the Plutonium marker could identify a reactor type and most likely its size. Different sizes indicated the ship's size. During his training, Chong had isolated the Plutonium marker in the lab from water samples provided. He was the only student to accurately identify the maker during the test.

He looked at the clock. It was 1648. He headed to the special comms room. He followed the instructions to fire up the system. The phone buzzed.

"Mr. Chong, the antenna is ready."

"Thank you, sir. I will call you after I am done."

Chong pressed the transmit button. It took just seconds for the connection to be made. The monitor blinked on and the face of his controller appeared.

"Chong, congratulations, you have passed your first test. I am sending you an email with further instructions. You are not to print out the email, but only view it on the monitor. The message will auto erase after viewing. Are there any questions?"

"No sir. I will report each day, Chong out." He pressed the off button. He saw a message appear on the monitor. It was straight forward and simple. He was to use the radiation and sonar machines twice daily, 0900 and 1600. If any alarm sounded, it would indicate that one of the systems had detected something. The results would be recorded and sent to the comms room automatically. When he connected to his controller, the information would be auto sent.

The manual indicated how to log the information. It would require no more than ten minutes per session to record the data. He would be able to see the data, but he did not have the equipment to display the results in any meaningful form. All he would know was the data had been recorded and sent. Someone else would be responsible to diagnose the data. His first day was done. The situation screen showed the sub's location eight-hundred miles West of the Philippines.

HMAS Robertson

Lt. Randolph Brice sat in his small cabin contemplating his situation. Not good. He was trapped on a sinking ship with a crew that had no discipline and a drunken skipper.

He got up and went to the bridge. Surely there was a land line connected or a cell phone. He searched but found nothing that he could make a call to his boss in Canberra.

Brice left the bridge and made his way on deck. He saw seaman McDuffie speaking to a crewman. He waited a moment to allow McDuffie time to acknowledge his presence.

McDuffie continued to carry on the conversation. Brice coughed and got their attention. McDuffie immediately turned and came running up to Brice. "Sir is there anything I can do to assist you?"

"Yes, I need a phone. I couldn't find one on the bridge."

"No sir. The Captain had it removed. He said if anyone wanted to talk to him, they would have to do it in person."

"I see. How does the crew communicate with their families?"

"We take turns using one of the crew's cell phone. We pay a dollar for five minutes."

"Good, I need that cell phone now." Brice noticed seaman McDuffie look down. "Is there a problem with my request?"

"No sir, the phone is being charged at the moment. I will bring it to you after it is fully charged. You have to climb to the top of the mast to get a signal." McDuffie looked up at the ladder welded to the side of the mast. The mast went up at least twenty meters.

Brice shook his head. "I'm not climbing up there to use the phone. Take me into town. I'll go to the officer's club and use the phone."

"Sir, the officer's club burned down a month ago. I'm not sure where the officers meet now. You could use a phone on one of the ships in port. I know a couple of guys on one of the ships."

"Okay, let's get moving." McDuffie looked like a deer in the headlights.

"Sir, we no longer have transportation. The Shore Patrol came and took it away. It seems it went missing from a family's back yard."

"This is totally unbelievable. Okay, as soon as that phone is charged, I want to use it. Do you understand?"

"Yes sir. I'll bring it to your cabin." McDuffie hurried off as fast as possible without breaking into a run.

Naval HQ, Canberra

The Admiral called a meeting of his staff. They were all seated in the conference room. The Admiral stood.

"Gentlemen, we have a situation. It appears the Chinese have stepped up their presence in our waters. We need some way to detect where they are and what type of ships they have deployed. Do I have any suggestions?" There were no hands. "So, none of you have a clue what we should do about the Chinese roaming off our shores?"

One commodore raised his hand. "Sir, in light of the AUKUS deal being made public, I suggest we immediately outfit a patrol ship with the latest detection equipment."

The Admiral looked at the commodore a few seconds. "And what will that accomplish? We already know they are here with Submarines, destroyers and maybe even a battleship. We know what they have and the question is what do we do about it?"

A Captain raised his hand. "Sir, what would happen if we sent out bogus signals from a patrol ship, similar to what a nuclear sub would make? They may think twice about messing with us. According to the Yanks, The Chinese don't know if the Yanks have sent any of their latest subs to the South Pacific."

The Admiral stared at the Captain. "You stay, all the remainder of you go back to your business."

The staff shuffled out of the room. "Sir, I hope that did not offend you." He stared down at the table top.

"No Captain, I'm not offended. I'm just amazed that no one else had anything to offer. I like your idea. How do we go about doing this?"

"Sir, we will need a ship to deliver the fake signals that has a low chance of having a signature that has been captured by the Chinese. I remember a course in the training program for sonar operators. It sent out signatures of nearly every ship afloat. It was so real; many experienced sonar operators were fooled. All we need is a low priority ship to install the right equipment."

The Captain's cell phone buzzed. He looked at the display. "Sir it's Lt. Brice? Sir he is one of your staff we sent to replace officers out with the Covid-19 virus. He was deployed to the HMAS Robertson."

The Admiral nodded. The Captain pressed the answer key. "This is Captain Thomson." He listened for a few seconds. "Hold on Brice. I want to put you on speaker. The Admiral is here with me. Please start over."

"Sir, I am on the HMAS Robertson. The ship is a wreck. It is a thirty year old destroyer that's spent more time in the ship yard than at sea. It is tied up at a wharf near Perth. The skipper is not in condition to command due to, uh the virus, and nothing on the ship works. The deck gun is rusted in position; the long range sensors were declared shot and must be completely replaced, these top secret devices are made in China. The engines are being overhauled but parts are not available. The crew is not disciplined. Sir I would like to be recalled?

The Admiral smiled. "Brice, I want you on the next available flight back to Canberra. Let Captain Thomson know your plans."

"Sir, I will send a text with my flight information, Brice out." The connection was broken.

"Captain, we just found our ship and point man. I want you in charge of the operation, make it top secret. Get all the technical information available on how the school uses the fake signals and convert it to be used on the HMAS Robertson. Have Brice trained in its use."

"Yes sir." The Captain left the Admiral sitting at the conference table smiling.

Chapter Twelve

Realm Hotel

McClusky/Jenkins sat at the bar in the fancy lounge. There were few people, mostly men. Louse sat smiling at Jenkins. She thought maybe she was falling for the rich man.

They had concluded the changes to the proposal for the purchase of the French software company. They were to meet with the chairman at 0900 tomorrow to sign the deal. She wondered if she was expected to stay the night again. She didn't mind, it was fantastic. She would wait and see how the evening progressed.

She had emailed the document to his legal people or so she thought. If all went well, tomorrow she would be well off with half a million in the bank.

McClusky phoned his office in London to alert them the purchase document was on its way. He had no idea what they would do with it. He sipped his single malt Scotch. He saw two men come into the lounge. It was Kluso and the unknown man.

Jenkins turned so his face was not seen. He was not sure if Kluso knew him by sight or not. He didn't want to take any chances. He still had not heard back on the identity of the man with Kluso.

"Louise, I have a dinner engagement with some clients, can you be back about 2300?"

She smiled. This was perfect. She needed a change of clothes and her makeup kit. "Sure, I'm looking forward to it." She had on her happy face.

Jenkins smiled and continued to keep an eye on Kluso. He was thinking, *what the hell is he doing here anyway?* The French are out, period. There is nothing they can do, or maybe there is something going on.

He observed Kluso and friend take a table on the far side of the room. It was perfect for McCluskey's purposes. "I've got to run, see you at 2300. He patted her hand, signed the tab to his room and made his way out of the room without passing by Kluso's table.

Hotel Omni

McClusky entered the dining room and looked around. He spotted Donovan seated at a table with the NCIS agent. He walked over and pulled out a chair. "Nice to see you guys again."

Donovan looked up from his menu. "Hi, we just sat down. Would you like a drink?"

"Yes thank you. A single malt Scotch would be nice."

Donovan motioned for a waiter to take the drinks order. "We have been busy trying to coordinate with the Aussie intelligence agency. They are playing it close to the chest. They claim to have an air tight facility for the construction of the sub. We were politely told they would give us information if we cooperated." McClusky raised an eyebrow.

"Yes, this may be a small country, but they have a world class intelligence force. By the way, I saw Kluso and friend at my hotel a few minutes ago. There has to be something up. Their loss of the contract for the construction of the sub is a done deal. So they are here on a mission of unknown matters." Donovan looked at Rosenberg and back at McClusky. "Now that is interesting."

Tina raised an eyebrow but jumped right in."The Navy still has a contract with the software company supplying crucial top secret software," said Rosenberg.

"Well, that may not be a fact in a few days. We have made an offer to purchase the company. The deal is to be completed tomorrow morning. That will mean the French will no longer have any ties to the construction. All but four of the staff are local. The four French staff will not be employed after tomorrow," said McClusky.

"Well that is welcomed news. We were in a quandary as how to fix that problem. Are you sticking around after he deal goes down?"

"Only a few days until our manager is on the scene. My job is complete. I'll be returning to London."

"Since you mentioned Kluso, we are sticking around a while longer. Kluso and friend are a bit worrisome. There has to be something going on. We originally suspected Kluso was in with the MSS to interfere with the new sub. But with the secure assembly facility, that does not seem feasible," said Rosenberg.

"Well, I would not underestimate Kluso, he's been around the block a few times," said McClusky.

Their dinner arrived, the conversation changed from business to other matters. After the meal was finished, McClusky left and returned to his suite. Louise was already there.

Canberra ASIO

Mason Livingston sat at his desk thumbing through profiles of all the workers at the secret N-5 building. It was a long boring task. There were over a thousand workers assigned to that building on three shifts. His phone buzzed.

"Livingston here." He listened. Grabbed a pencil and wrote down a name. "Thanks, keep monitoring and when you get the evidence, let me know." He disconnected the call.

So, there is a spy in the N-5 building. With the tight security, he was interested in how the spy would take pictures. He found the folder with the name Yen Lee.

He read all the interview notes and the qualifications of the man. It seems he got in while the sub was still under the French construction crew. He just showed up and applied as a master welder, the one job short workers. The human resources people did only a surface check on his background. When they found his name in the union files, they assumed he was legit. The paper showed Lee was assigned to area M.

He phoned the special group responsible for surveillance equipment. They were instructed to install cameras inside N-5 focused on the M section of the sub.

The feed from the cameras was routed to a special IP address on a secure server in Canberra.

Livingston sent an email to the two watchers informing them of the secret IP address. They could monitor Lee in real time.

Naval HQ

Lt. Brice grabbed his carryall from the overhead bin. The flight had taken six hours from Perth to Canberra. It was an Air Force 737.

A sergeant spotted him and introduced himself as his temporary aide. They climbed into a jeep and headed for the Russell Complex.

Brice showed his ID to the guard who recognized him. The sergeant escorted him through a maze of halls and stairs. They ended up on the top floor in top brass territory. He had never been in this area of the complex. He was escorted into a conference room.

The door opened at the far end of the room and a Captain entered. Brice jumped to attention and saluted the Captain. "Please be seated Lieutenant. My name is Captain Thomson. We spoke briefly on the phone on Tuesday.

"Yes sir. I am so thankful you got me off that ship. It is a disaster."

The Captain stared at Brice. "Well that may be a short reprieve. We have a special project for you involving the HMAS Robertson." Brice jerked at the announcement he was still involved with the wretched ship.

"Sir, what sort of project?"

"Son, this is top secret. Only you me and the Admiral will know of its existence. The HMAS Robertson is to play a vital role in protecting our country. Your role is to make sure the project goes off without a hitch. You will first attend a special school on a top secret device and other related equipment."

Brice sat with glazed eyes. His hope of forgetting the Robertson was dashed. "Sir the ship is not sea worthy and the captain is not fit for duty."

"I know that. That is why you are promoted as of today and will be the Captain of The Robertson. You will oversee the replacement of any crew you deem not compatible with your mission. You will also be responsible for reporting directly to me and the Admiral. You will have an executive officer fully familiar with this class of ship. You will not be required to manage the ship."

"Sir what is my mission?"

"You are to confuse any ship trying to enter our waters by sending fake sonar signatures. You will send a host of different signatures to appear as if a fleet of ships and subs were in the waters near any foreign ships. You will learn more of this as the days go on. A handpicked crew, by the new executive officer is on their way to the Robertson as I speak to install and replace all necessary equipment to accomplish your mission. That includes engines, deck gun, and a thorough overhaul. The Perth ship yard has given the Robertson the highest priority. "

Brice only hoped the thing didn't sink on its way to the ship yard, about five kilometers, may as well be going to the moon.

Building N-5

Yen Lee went through the protocol of changing his clothes and joining Archer in the hallway and waited for his boss to open the door. This would be his first day actually working on the new sub.

The door swung open and his boss waved all through. He told them to go to their assigned work stations and begin work. Lee and Archer went to the platform connecting the sub to the work area. The large painted M was very prominent.

Archer was reading the assignment papers. "It says we are to weld the four external plates in place before any work is done on the Hot Box."

Lee nodded and they examined the plates marked with an M. Lee picked up the mobile phone and pressed the alert button. A gruff voice came over the phone. "What's your position?"

Lee looked at Archer who was smiling. "M" said Lee. "We have four plates to weld. We will need to have them hoisted into position and we can tack them in place before the final weld."

"Okay, you are second in line this morning. Be sure to mark the plate's one through four so I will know the order to pick them up. Crane out."

Archer laughed, "Seems he's of the old school. Let's sort out the plates and mark them for the crane operator."

The two carefully examined each plate. There were some differences but someone had already marked them one to four.

Lee read the assignment papers carefully and compared the specs to the physical plates. "Number 3 is actually number four and four should be three. They had been marked wrong."

Archer raised an eyebrow. "I think we should report this to the boss before we change anything."

"Good idea. I'll call him over." Lee looked at the various work areas and finally spotted the boss three stations away. He waved until the boss noticed and waved back. The boss made his way to the M work station.

"Okay, what's the problem?"

Lee looked at Archer and nodded. Archer showed the specs for plates three and four to the boss. "These are marked backwards. I just wanted your approval before I changed the order."

The boss looked at the plates and took out a tape measure. "Looks like you are correct. Some jerk in the other building had marked these before we moved the boat to here. Good catch men. Remark them and get them in place." He walked off and joined another work group.

Lee measured the third plate and confirmed the number should be four. He sprayed over the three and put a four and on the fourth plate he made it number three. Archer nodded. "Well we have to wait our turn for the crane. I think I'll use the facilities. Lee and Archer headed to the facilities area. Lee said he would wait on the bench outside.

Lee positioned his leg to the proper position to get a full length shot of the boat. Archer returned and they walked to their station just as the crane operator announced he was moving to their station.

The lunch time whistle blue. All the teams ate their lunch at their work stations. Thirty minutes was allotted for lunch.

Observers

The two observers sat staring at their screens. The view of the huge room was perfect. They would be able to observe Lee in detail. So far they had not seen anything out of the ordinary.

They saw Lee and his coworker take a break. Lee remained on the bench outside of the facilities. He only stared at other teams. His partner came out and they walked back to their station.

The lunch whistle blew and the two sat down on their scaffold and ate their lunch. They didn't talk. They observed Lee and his mate temporally weld four plates into position until they could properly weld them permanently. The shift end whistle blew. They watched him put his tools into the tool box He placed his helmet and gloves in a neat pile and picked them up along with the tool box. Archer did the same. They joined the others going to the locker room for their street clothes. The observers switched cameras to the one in the locker room. Lee sat on a bench and removed his shoes and placed his tool box, helmet and gloves into the locker and changed into his street clothes, put his shoes back on and left the building. The exterior camera showed him mount his motor cycle and leave the car park. Ten minutes later Lee entered his apartment. He went to his bedroom and changed into sweats. He placed his shoes on a small shelf in the back of the closet. Lee pressed a small button on the side of the shoe that activated a blue tooth device.

"Well, it looks like our number one suspect did nothing out of the ordinary today," said the female.

"Yes, I only hope we are successful in getting a breach tomorrow. Do you think he will try to report anything to his handler?"

"I suggest we take turns watching him until he goes to bed. We may get lucky. I'll go first," said the female.

Lee fixed himself a simple meal of rice and pork. He turned on his TV and watched the news.

It seemed the Covid-19 pandemic was now in full force. He turned off the TV and turned on his laptop.

"Hey, he's on his computer. He just logged into FaceBook. He's typing a message into Facebook Messenger."

They both watched the message being typed. Then a picture of the sub appeared. He pressed the send key. Within a few seconds the Like appeared.

The photo file deleted itself as soon as the message was sent.

"What the Hell. Where did that picture come from? We didn't see him take any pictures. There could not have been a camera hidden in his clothes, we saw him change into the provided jump suit," said the male.

"It's like he had the picture already on his hard drive. But that is impossible. He had only worked in that building one day. His phone was in his locker. We observed him all the time."

The female said, "Somehow, he managed to take a picture and upload it to his computer. He never inserted a thumb drive. We need to examine his router and determine if anything other than the Internet was accessed."

"I'm on it. I'm inside the router. There are three devices on his private network, his laptop, a printer and some unknown device," said the male.

"Can you determine what the unknown device is?"

"No, it does not have an IP address. It must be Blue Tooth. It looks like a phone, but much weaker. I'm trying to access it. It has a password."

"If it is Blue Tooth, then the router must be custom built with a Blue Tooth receiver. That still does not explain how the picture got into the device. We can't arrest him without hard evidence that he took the picture. At this point we obviously missed something."

"I'm uploading what we have to Canberra. I'm not going to speculate how the picture was taken. Do you think there could be two, one taking the pictures and one sending the data to Beijing? Are we watching the wrong person?"

Chapter Thirteen

Perth Ship Yard

The HMAS Robertson was pulled by two tug boats. The Robertson looked sad and ready for the scrap yard. The poor thing was listing more than ten degrees as it cleared the port entrance. The pumps keeping it afloat were straining.

The new crew had been driven to the ship yard in a bus. The safety officer from the ship yard said it was too dangerous for them to remain on board.

The tugs took over an hour to get the Robertson into the dry dock. It was just before noon on Wednesday. The Commodore in charge of the ship yard had gotten orders directly from the Vice Admiral of the Navy. "Fix the damn thing as fast as possible."

The Commodore immediately summoned his best team. He explained the priority and said it was top secret. A new crew and Captain would be arriving shortly to assist in the installation of some top secret equipment. There were over one hundred men assigned to the near impossible task of overhauling the Robertson.

The water was pumped from the dry dock and men began to crawl all over the ship. The Yanks working on the engine had just received word the parts for the engines had arrived from Iowa. They were ready to go into action and started installing and testing the engines. The lead Yank had received his orders earlier from Langley.

The man from Spain was no longer needed. The equipment ordered from China was canceled. The old equipment he had been working on had been removed and replaced with a device custom made in Australia. The lead on the electronics team had received his orders from Canberra. A crate with new top secret equipment was due to arrive Saturday. The men from NUF were told their new deck gun was arriving on Monday.

The place turned into a bee hive of activity. The noise was deafening. There were over fifty men with electric sanders removing all the rust. Most wore masks because of the dust. The bilge leak causing the ship to list was repaired.

By Wednesday of the following week, the ship began to look like new. The new crew had arrived and was giving the interior a through scrubbing. The new executive officer, Lt. Tom Lance, had everything on the bridge replaced. Seaman McDuffie was told to remain in the crew. He was to see that the Captain's quarters was put into top condition as well as the Executive Officer's. McDuffie would be given new orders as soon as Captain Brice arrived.

The old Captain and crew were told to be prepared for new assignments in Darwin. They would be bused to Darwin in a few days. It would take four to five days. The old Captain was seen at a local liquor store stocking up for the long ordeal.

Captain Brice took intense classes on the top secret Aussie equipment. He was told the equipment was being installed on the HMAS Robertson and would be ready when he returned.

Brice absorbed the techniques fast and surprised his Aussie teachers on how fast he took to the concept. He had one more day of classes before he was to return to Perth. He had been gone for five weeks. He was told the overhaul of the Robertson had only a week remaining to be complete.

Watchers

The two watchers were concerned about their inability to determine how the uploaded photo was taken. If they arrested Lee now, they could not prove he took the photo. There was zero evidence he took the photo. They all but ruled out a second person. Even if a second person took the picture, how did they upload it to the router? Blue Tooth range was only a few meters.

No one had visited Lee and they had scanned the apartments on either side, above and below and found only a retired postal worker, two high school teachers and a policeman, none had computers. Their conclusion was there was no second person. So, that leaves Lee. He somehow took the picture.

Day two.

The watchers booted up their laptops and waited and stared at the empty locker room. Ten minutes later, Lee appeared on their screens opening his locker. He went through the procedure of placing his cell phone, wallet and some coins into the wicker basket as the watchers observed closely. Lee placed his lunch bag on the bench in full sight. "Could the camera be in his lunch bag?" asked the female.

"I don't think so, he has not touched the bag."

Lee removed his shoes and outer clothing and donned his work clothes and put his shoes back on. He removed his welding helmet, gloves and tool box from the locker. Archer was a few meters away doing the same. Once Lee had completed redressing, he grabbed his lunch bag and closed his locker then headed to the hallway to wait for his boss to open the assembly room door.

"Could he have a camera in his tool box?" Asked the female.

"I don't think so. Security randomly checks the lockers and they only got them yesterday. He would have to conceal the camera on his person to stow it in the tool box. We observed his every move, he never touched the tool box. We saw no action that would have given him time stow the camera and take the picture. There has to be some special type of camera technology involved here."

"Let's replay today's recording and look at the scene from the perspective that a camera is hidden someplace but the change of clothes does not reveal its location."

The recording started from the moment Lee entered the locker room. The first thing Lee did was to remove his light jacket and hang it up in the locker. They stopped the recording. The female studied the frame. "If the camera is in the jacket, he made no move to remove it." She pressed a key and the recording continued.

Lee was observed taking off his shirt and pants. Not once did he remove anything from any of the garments except his loose change, wallet and cell phone. Lee sat down and removed his shoes. He reached into the locker and removed the jump suit. It was clear he did not remove anything from his clothes hanging inside the locker. He sat down to put on his shoes.

"That's it!" The male replayed the recording from the closing of the locker. "The camera must be in the shoes. They are the only thing that was not exchanged. He wore his street shoes into the assembly room."

The female sat looking at the recording as Lee put on his shoes. "They look like the standard issued shoes for the workers. Let's play yesterday's recording and see if he somehow uses his shoes to take the picture." They punched up the recording from yesterday. They observed Lee following his work mate to the restroom area. Lee sat on a bench outside and waited. He crossed his legs. "He didn't touch his shoes. How would he activate a camera without touching his shoes? This is a dead end." They switched to the live camera in the assembly room.

They continued to observe Lee and Archer work through the morning. There was no opportunity for Lee to take a picture. Lunch time arrived.

The screen showed Archer and Lee stop work for lunch. Each had a lunch bag sitting on the scaffold platform. They sat to eat their lunch. Lee took a sandwich from his bag and a bottle of water. He ate quietly and placed the empty bottle and the sandwich wrapper back into the bag. They each pitched their empty lunch bags into a bin on the platform.

Chapter Fourteen

Lofgren

Kluso tapped a message into a satellite cell phone. He pressed the send key. Within a few seconds he received a message back. He smiled and placed the Sat Phone in his back pack. He picked up the in-house phone and called Lofgren's room. "I'm headed to the restaurant; if you want to come with me, meet me in the bar in ten minutes." Lofgren acknowledged the invitation and they arrived in the bar at the same time.

"I'm starved. Let's eat and discuss our mission," said Kluso.

They were seated at a table and ordered. Kluso saw a couple on the far side of the room. He thought he recognized the man, but did not get a good look at his face. The woman was seated with her back to him.

"So, what is our mission?" asked Lofgren. Kluso looked up from his meal.

"You don't know?"

"I was told certain things but I'm not sure what we are doing." He looked into Kluso's eyes.

"Well, I think it's about time you know what we are doing here. I do not understand why you were sent here. What is your specialty?"

"I'm a cryptologist. I work for the cyber division of the foreign office." Kluso sat back in his chair.

"A cryptologist? What does a cryptologist do?"

"My specialty is Chinese. I usually monitor transmissions from and to their embassy. If the message has been encrypted, I decode it."

"Where do you send it after you decode it?"

"I'm not sure. I type the decoded message into a software program and press the submit button. I have no idea who or where the message is read."

Kluso sat digesting what Lofgren had said. "I will get permission to discuss our mission with you. I was not told what your function was to be on this assignment. I'll be right back."

Kluso got up and went up to his room. He removed the Sat Phone and punched in a special number.

"Sir, I have a question. Why is Lofgren on this assignment and what am I to tell him?" Kluso listened. "I see. Well this should have been sorted out before we left France. I will bring him up to date." Kluso punched off the call. He thought, *as the Yanks say, this is a real SNAFU.* He replaced the phone into his backpack and returned to the restaurant.

"Well, I was given permission to explain what we are doing and what your role in the matter is all about." He looked into Lofgren's eyes. *The man has no idea what he is doing.* "I am assigned the mission of finding out what the Chinese are doing about the Aussie's building a nuclear sub." You are to assist me in translating any messages we can detect. I'm not sure how we are to do that, but I have a feeling you do." Kluso stared at Lofgren.

Lofgren licked his lips and nodded his head. "Yes, I brought classified equipment to eavesdrop on any messages to and from the Chinese Australian Embassy. I have no idea where the Chinese Embassy is located."

Kluso sat staring at the man. *Bloody hell, the poor chap is totally helpless.* "After we finish our meal, I'll show you to the Chinese Embassy across the road from this hotel. How close do you have to be to detect any messages?"

"As long as I can see their satellite dish, I can monitor their traffic. The distance doesn't matter"

"Good, our rooms overlook their building and there is a forest of dishes and antenna on top of the building. Let's get your equipment set up and see what is happening." Lofgren nodded and they left for his room.

An hour later, Lofgren had his equipment setup and tested. "The device is working and there is a stream of messages being transmitted at the moment. All will be recorded in the device for playback and deciphering. What am I to do with the unencrypted messages?"

Kluso shook his head. "For the moment, give them to me. If you believe something should be uploaded to Paris, then do it. Can you make out what the messages say?"

"Yes, they are using the same code as in Paris. It appears to be a relay from a Facebook user someplace in Australia and then uploaded to a specific IP address in Beijing. They are using FaceBook as a means to post messages. That is very secure. Anyone monitoring the source will not be able to determine where the message is going. Unless the person monitoring is a Facebook friend or knows the source's Facebook name, there is a zero chance the recipient of the message can be identified. By using the Australian Facebook version, only someone in Australia can see the posting. There is an image also included. It will take the computer a few minutes to sort out the pixels, but the message is very short. It says **the assembly has been moved to a secure location known as N-5**. Here comes the image, it looks like a ship under construction."

"So, if I understand, somebody is posting a message on Facebook with an image that only someone in the Chinese Embassy, in Australia can see and that person would have to know the senders Facebook name and also be a friend."

"Yes, and then that person receiving the message can then send it on to anyone with an IP address on the internet, that's how we are getting it."

"The time is 2000. We should monitor the messages at this time every day. In this business, operatives usually communicate at the same time every day. Whatever else is being received and transmitted by the embassy should be recorded also.

Lofgren nodded he understood. "The device will auto unencrypt any messages and post a notification for me to read. I do not have to be sitting here all the time."

"Good, well we have learned the MSS has a spy within the assembly building. We can monitor the progress of the sub."

Kluso had an idea of how to use this information. It would defiantly slow the project and put doubts in the Yanks and British overseers that they are secure. The MSS will be really pissed, but hey, it's the game.

Chapter Fifteen

The New HMAS Robertson

Newly commissioned Captain Randolph Brice walked down the stairs of the Qantas 737 carrying a briefcase and spotted McDuffie standing near the exit. McDuffie wore civvies. Most of the passengers wore masks including Brice, but since he was the only one on the plane who wore a dress Navy uniform he was easy to identify. McDuffie waved and waited until Brice pulled his baggage from the carousel.

"Welcome back Captain. Things have changed and I am happy to report the ship is like new. You will not recognize the Robertson."

"Thanks for meeting me. Are any of the old crew members still assigned to the Robertson?"

"Yes sir, me and two others. We are the only ones. The others are on their way to Darwin. The new crew fits the ship like they were born on it."

"Great. There will be quite a lot of work to do before we can leave port. So, let's get going. Uh, I hope you have better transportation than the last time."

"Yes sir. I used one of the new jeeps assigned to our ship. I'm sure you will approve." With that McDuffie turned, picked up Brice's carryall and headed towards the car park. Brice followed along carrying his briefcase.

Good to Captain Thomas' word, Brice saw a new jeep with an enclosed cab and had the HMAS Robertson stenciled on the side. Brice smiled. *So Captain Thomas was not kidding when he said the ship would be completely upgraded with all new equipment.*

McDuffie put the bag in the back and started the engine. "Sir, would you like for me to place your case in the back?"

"No, that will not be necessary. This is a great jeep." McDuffie noticed the handcuff attached to the case for the first time.

"Sir, we have four of these assigned to us, all with air-conditioning. Lieutenant Lance is doing a great job getting the ship ready for you. I made sure your quarters were completely cleaned, painted and outfitted with new carpet." Brice smiled. *Maybe this will work out.*

McDuffie drove the jeep down the pier and stopped at a gangway with the ship's name painted on the canvas sides.

Brice stared at the ship. "Wow, this is not our ship?

"Yes sir this is our ship. Good as new. I was told you have some things to do concerning the new bridge equipment. I'm to take you directly to the bridge."

Brice walked up the gangway. He observed several men busy working on some strange looking equipment on the aft deck. "Seaman, what are those men working on?"

McDuffie looked over where Brice was staring. "Sir I'm not sure. I've never seen any of the devices before. The ship's crew is not allowed on that part of the deck." McDuffie motioned for a seaman standing at the top of the gangway to approach. "Take this baggage to the Captain's quarters." The man nodded, "Yes Chief" and picked up Brice's carryall and disappeared through a hatch.

"Have you received a promotion since I left?"

"Yes sir, I am now a Chief Petty Officer. With a smile, he motioned for Brice to follow him to the bridge.

Bridge

Brice was shocked at what he saw on the bridge. Everything was new. The small room that had contained the electronic equipment was now outfitted with a chair pushed under a counter top like desk attached to the equipment rack. The equipment looked very small compared to the old rack of stuff. The door was also new, and contained security devices. He observed the same type of controls he had used in school

"McDuffie, who has access to this room and why is it open?"

"Sir, with the exception of the installation crew, no one but you and Lt. Lance are authorized. The Lieutenant unlocked the door only moments ago when he saw you board the ship."

"Where is Lt. Lance?"

"I'm right behind you, Captain." Brice jumped at the sound of a voice behind him. "Sorry for startling you, but I had to give instructions to one of the crew before joining you on the bridge."

"Lieutenant Lance, it is a pleasure to meet you. I have been briefed on your extensive knowledge of this class of vessel." They shook hands. Lance saw the handcuffed briefcase. "As for me, I've very little experience on this ship. I have some work to perform in the electronics room. So if you would excuse me for now. Let's have dinner together and catch up on our mission." Lance saluted Brice and left the bridge.

"Sir is there anything else I can do for you," asked McDuffie.

"No thank you Chief. I will be here for the next hour or so." McDuffie saluted, closed the door and left Brice alone in the small electronics room.

Brice stood in the room looking at the array of screens and other equipment. He placed the briefcase on the desk top. He entered four digits on the handcuff's small display and the handcuff sprung open. There was a leather flap cover over a finger print detector that would open the case with his forefinger. He placed his finger on the detector and the case lid clicked open.

A leather bound book and a thumb drive was removed and placed on the desktop. The thumb drive was inserted in the USB receptacle on the equipment rack. He typed a code on the keyboard and placed his right eye on the scanner. The screens lit up and asked for a voice confirmation.

"I am Captain Randolph Brice, Serial number A98-T45."

"Welcome aboard Captain. You have control."

Brice was still uncomfortable with the latest AI computer. The thing seemed actually alive. He downloaded the thumb drive and the screen became active. A message was displayed; Transducers are off-line please bring all transducers on-line. Brice stared at the message. In school all he had to do was to tap a few keys and all was well. He tapped the keys, the message remained.

Brice sat for a few seconds staring at the various screens and checking the information displayed. He saw a folded piece of paper tucked under one of the control devices. It was a hand written note.

The Transducers will not be operational until Friday. Please do not attempt to use them until I have released the equipment to you. Signed: George Russell, Rathon Corporation. Sydney.

Brice used his mouse to click on shutdown. The computer asked him, "Captain are you sure you want to shutdown?"

"Yes shutdown now." The computer began to display shutdown information on the main screen.

There was a knock on the door. Brice waited until all the screens went dark then reached and opened the door. Standing outside was a tall man with unruly blond hair. "Sir, I am George Russell. I'm sorry I was not here to welcome you and explain the status of the equipment."

"Mr. Russell, I'm sure you had better things to do than to cater to me. I'm not sure of the status of the equipment."

"Sir, we are installing the Transducer array today. I will calibrate the system and tomorrow you will be able to run all the equipment."

"What is the Transducer array?"

"It is the dome like device you see on the deck near the back of the ship. The dome is to contain all the devices in a water proof environment. The dome will be installed mid ship under the water. It contains the transmitters to send out the signatures you select on the console here. If the signature requires a radiation component, the array will automatically release the programmed amount directly in the water. The joy stick will turn the array to the compass point you select. It can move in 180 degree arcs. The position is displayed on the situation screen. You can also tell the computer to move and select any signature you want to broadcast. The computer is also capable of analyzing incoming signatures and advising you of possible solutions.

"Does the computer have a name?"

Russell stood staring at Brice. After a few seconds he grinned, "Yes, her name is Mandy, but you can rename it to anything you like. Just go into settings and select computer name."

"I'll shut down shop for now and give that some thought. Russell nodded and left the room. Brice stowed the briefcase in a lockable drawer under the desk top. It would only open with his finger print. He closed the door to the room and pressed the lock key. The door made a metallic sound as it locked.

Brice looked around the bridge and liked what he saw. This duty may just turn out to be not so bad after all. He left the bridge and headed to his quarters. He was a bit apprehensive taking the Captain's quarters. He knew nothing about giving orders to maneuver the ship or anything else concerning running the ship. That would be Lieutenant Lance's domain.

He went down the stairs to the corridor containing the officer's quarters. He saw that it was brightly lit. There was no mildew smell and the bulkheads looked freshly painted. He saw his name neatly painted on his door.

He reached and turned the latch handle. The door swung open without a squeak. He entered and was shocked at the size of the quarters. It had to be at least four times the size of his former quarters. There was an alcove that contained a laptop computer, a screen with the ship's vital status information and a new iPhone was lying on the desk with a note.

Sir you will not have to climb the mast to use this baby.

McDuffie.

Laughing, *McDuffie does have a sense of humor after all.* Brice picked up the phone and examined the signal. It had three bars. They must have installed signal repeaters within the ship.

His carryall was on a standard size bed. He decided to get out of the dress uniform and put on his new khakis with captain's bars on the collar. The closet was huge compared to his old one. He hung up his uniform and donned the khakis and put away his other clothing items in the drawers built into the closet.

The clock on the wall displayed two different times. One was Canberra and the other was labeled as Zulu. He knew that meant local ship's time. It read 1706. He looked around satisfied with his new digs and headed topside. It would be dinner time in an hour. It was enough time to take a quick walk around.

The crew from NUF had almost completed the installation of the new deck gun. He recognized the lead man. He waved and the man waved back. Brice approached the man. "Looks like you guys have almost completed the installation."

"Well, almost means a couple of more days. I don't know who you talked to, but thanks. The gun and parts arrived four days after you left. Thanks." He turned and went back to work.

Brice smiled and walked back towards the stern. Just as he arrived at the walkway to the stern, two marines with side arms stood in his way. "Sir, this is a restricted area. Only authorized personnel are allowed." The one speaking looked into Brice's eyes.

"Solder, I am the Captain of this vessel, I think that qualifies as authorized." He pointed at the bars on his collar. The two marines looked at each other. One keyed his radio and turned to be private. Brice couldn't hear what the marine said but he heard the response. "Damnit, he is the captain. He is authorized to see anything."

"Sir, sorry but we only arrived here today for security."

"No apology necessary, just doing your job. Carry on." They both snapped to attention and saluted.

Brice saw a dome shaped object on the deck with two men working on something inside the dome. The dome was not much larger than a beach ball. He recognized one of the men to be Russell. He decided to not disturb their work. Two men in scuba gear were preparing for a dive. Brice figured they were to install the dome on the bottom of the ship. The ship was tied up at the pier and the divers would be in only thirty feet of water.

He walked to a hatch leading down towards the engine room and saw several men working on one of the six engines. One looked up. He smiled.

"Look who showed up, our savior. Thanks for whatever you did to uncork the delay in getting our engine parts. These babies are at one hundred percent now. My men and I will be departing in two days. We are to do a sea trial tomorrow. Thanks again." All the men nodded.

Brice waved and went back to the deck. He looked at his watch and headed toward the officer's mess, which on this vessel was the ward room.

Brice opened the door to the ward room. Three officers were seated around the small conference table. Lance looked up and stood along with the others at attention. "Sir welcome to the Robertson."

"Thank you Lieutenant. Everyone at ease and be seated. Except when we are in the presence of crew, we will skip the formality of saluting." He was offered a seat next to Lieutenant Lance.

"Captain, I would like to introduce you to your officers. This is Ensign Morgan and Ensign Brook. They will each take a shift on the bridge whenever I'm not on duty. I don't know if they told you, we are going on a sea trial tomorrow."

"Yes, the men working on the engines told me a short time ago. It's a pleasure to meet you and have your expertise. I'm sure you know, we have a top secret mission. Lieutenant Lance will be in total charge of the day to day functions of the ship. That includes all ship maneuvering orders. Now let's get down to dinner."

Lance smiled, "Sir, in your honor, tonight will be steak night. I hope that meets your approval. Our meals should be here any moment." As if on cue, the door opened and a seaman with a large tray placed four plates on the table containing large rib eye steaks and four bowls of salad greens. "Sir, call the mess when you want dessert." He turned and closed the door.

Brice dug into his steak. It was fantastic. The baked potato was perfect. When the dessert arrived, he couldn't believe they had baked Alaska. This is going to be a great assignment, he hoped.

Chapter Sixteen

Fu Win

The Fu Win was making good time plowing through the ocean. It had been only a week since it left the sub pen. The sub would remain submerged for security. Its location was now one hundred nautical miles west of Perth.

Chi Lu Chong was preparing his daily report to Beijing. The sonar alarm sounded. The screen showed three vessels. The computer identified two of the vessels as US destroyers. The third was not in the database. Chong notified the Captain immediately. The engines stopped and the sub went into silent running mode.

Chong recorded the signatures and included all in his report. The sub went to antenna depth and he pressed the transmit button. His screen showed a one line message. **Report received.**

Chong used the phone on the wall to notify the Captain he was done with the transmission.

The Fu Win slipped down to a depth of one hundred meters, a classified depth. Chong watched the sonar screen. The three vessels were still on the screen but the signal was getting weaker. After ten minutes the signals disappeared.

HMAS Robertson

The sea trials were in full swing. The Robertson sliced through the ocean at over forty-five knots. Off the bow were two American destroyers accompanying the Robertson. Brice sat in the small electronics room with George Russell who explained how most of the devices worked.

"Sir, this is the sonar gain control. You advance the control to the right and watch the graph. When the graph flattens you have reached maximum sensitivity."

"What happens if I advance past the optimum sensitivity?"

"The signal will degrade and be unidentifiable by the software."

An alarm went off. A signal was coming in. The two American destroyers were accounted for as blue icons on the screen, but this was a new signal and deep. It had to be a sub. The icon turned red.

Instinctively, Brice used his knowledge learned at the school in Canberra. He separated the new signal from the two destroyers accompanying the Robertson.

The computer began to digest the sonar signature. Brice adjusted the sensitivity until the graph went flat. The computer responded.

"The signature is at optimum. The sub is the Fu Win from the Chinese Navy. Depth is one hundred meters and speed is thirty five knots. Signature verified and recorded"

"Wow, I didn't expect to detect anything on this test run," said Brice.

The Russell looked surprised also. "The analysis algorithm worked perfectly. The sub seems to have slowed a bit. I figure they have detected us. Let's see what happens when we send out the signature of a US Battleship," said Brice.

Brice opened a window on the monitor with a list of US Battleships near Australia. He saw the nuclear battleship New Haven was supposed to be in Australian waters. He keyed in the ID code for the New Haven. The AI responded as the signature was beamed from the device on the ship's belly. A special device dispersed the radiation in the proper amount for a Battleship.

Brice's sonar screen showed the sub turn and head west at high speed. They had scared the sub away. The fake signature worked.

Fu Win

Chong sat at the receptor desk as the alarm sounded. He punched a button to silence the alarms. The screen showed the previously unidentified ship as the Battleship New Haven dead ahead. He picked up the phone to the Captain. "Sir the American Battleship New Haven is twenty-five kilometers ahead. It is moving in this direction." The sub suddenly turned and headed due west.

Chong sat looking at the screen as the sub sped away at nearly sixty knots. He watched the status screen. He was amazed at the speed and depth the Fu Win was capable of achieving. Within fifteen minutes the sonar screen lost track of the destroyers, but The radiation detector still showed a ship clearly as a nuclear powered battleship. He wondered why a US battleship was in Australian waters with only two destroyers as escorts. Maybe this was not a fluke.

Chapter Seventeen

Omni Hotel

Kluso sat still and appeared almost in a trance. Lofgren had no idea what was going on. He thought that Kluso had a seizure or heart attack. After a moment or two, Kluso coughed and looked almost normal. "Let's go snoop on the Chinese."

They arrived in Lofgren's room. The message light was blinking. Lofgren punched a few keys. The message displayed on the large flat screen.

To Lu Kuban: Australian Embassy
The Battle ship New Haven is in the area. The Fu Win will remain on station until further orders are received from Beijing. Advise our operative to not take any more pictures until ordered to do so.
Li Moag, Special MSS Envoy

Kluso reread the message. He was impressed. The MSS had a full network in place. They have comms to a sub and operatives in place. He did not want the MSS to find out he was monitoring their transmissions. He turned to Lofgren. "Is there a way the Chinese can detect our monitoring?"

"No, as long as we do not transmit on their frequency. We are completely passive and undetectable."

"The MSS operatives in Adelaide are using the internet and not radio transmission. We don't have access to their user name. If we were close to them, I could try to Blue Tooth into their system and piggy back on their connection. But that would be a long shot. All we can do is keep monitoring the local traffic to the Embassy."

Kluso nodded. Can you set up a fake email address and send an email with the picture of the sub under construction to the British MI-6 in London without exposing our set up?"

Lofgren though for a moment, "I can have the email relayed from our secure server in Toulon. I saved the image we intercepted and can easily attach it to the email. There are many fake email accounts already set up on a special server. Once the email is sent from one of the fake addresses it is auto deleted."

"Okay, I will type the message and you then attach he photo and send it."

Lofgren nodded. He pointed to the chair in front of a keyboard and screen. Kluso sat and began to type.

To: Col. McClusky, MI-6
The attached picture was intercepted and I thought you might be interested.
Eye-in-the-sky
Attachment: Pic1.jpg 235 kb

Lofgren attached the picture and sent the email. Kluso smiled. "That should keep them busy for a few days. I'll come by here at 0800 tomorrow morning and see what is happening." Kluso left Lofgren's room.

London MI-6

McClusky sat in his cubical reading the Times. His phone rang, he answered, "McClusky." He listened a few seconds. "Can you trace its origin?" He frowned. "I'll be right there." He folded his newspaper and headed for the comms room.

The comms room supervisor saw him enter. He motioned for McClusky to come over to his area. McClusky walked swiftly towards the desk with the supervisor. When he arrived there was a short message on one screen and a picture of a sub under construction on another.

"What the bloody hell. It's been less than a Month and someone has a spy already monitoring the construction and God knows what else. Where did the email come from?"

"Sir, it has a bogus IP address. Someone with some very sophisticated equipment sent this."

"What would happen if we tried to reply?" "Nothing, since the IP address is non-existent, it will be returned by the email server." McClusky stood looking at the picture. He thanked the supervisor and headed back to his cubical.

McClusky looked at the series of clocks on the wall. One was labeled Sydney. It was 0600 in Sydney and Canberra. He sat down and contemplated his next move. Someone wants him to know there is a spy in the secure assembly building. Someone has access to the spy's transmissions. Someone does not want to be identified. Someone knows how to hide in cyber space. This seems a lot like a Kluso event, but why? He picked up his paper and resumed reading. After about an hour, he folded his paper and placed it in the dust bin. He looked at the Sydney time. It was 0705. He took his Sat Phone from a drawer and scanned the contact list. He saw Donovan's name and pressed the call button.

Canberra

Donovan was dressing when his phone buzzed. He looked at the display. He did not recognize the number. "Hello?" He wrinkled his forehead as he listened. "Damn that is not good news. I assume your people tried a trace?" His lips curled downward as he listened. "Send me the picture and I'll run it past the Aussies to find where the camera had to be to take the shot." He listened a few more seconds and closed the call.

He looked at the time. His flight was in the afternoon and many hours away. He had most of the day to run this up the pole. There was really not much he could do. He forgot to ask McClusky if the Aussies had been notified. He would phone Livingston and find out if he had received a call from McClusky. It was a bit early. He would call after breakfast. Donovan knew the Aussies discovered the spy and had people watching. What he didn't know was the significance of having a spy in the assembly building? Was the MSS going to try to sabotage the assembly? Were the Chinese that paranoid? Who was the mysterious email sender?

Chinese Embassy

The comms room of the Chinese Embassy was in the basement and well shielded. It was swept twice daily for bugs and cameras.

Zio Ping sat at her station monitoring various transmissions. There was nothing out of the ordinary. She had been told by her supervisor there was suspicious activity concerning the secret sub base in Adelaide. A burst transmission had been detected from the area but was unable to be captured. She was to capture any signals not normally present.

After observing for four hours nothing had appeared. She would be relieved from duty in fifteen minutes. The stress was causing her a pounding headache.

A screen suddenly became active. It was the satellite receiver. It had just picked up a burst transmission from someplace unknown. She quickly pressed the display button. The transmission was captured the moment the receiver detected the burst. It was short, about four seconds. She ran the signal through the decryption computer. The message was in a cipher not in the computer. She pressed the supervisor alert button.

She heard the supervisor running through the room. He came behind her. "Show me!"

Zio pointed to the screen. "Damn, we'll have to upload this to Beijing. We don't have the latest software to decode.

"Yes sir." Zio pressed a few keys and the captured signal was on its way to the super secret location of the MSS on the outskirts of Beijing.

HMAS Robertson

Brice sat in the tiny room with Russell. They were convinced the fake signatures worked. The sub had slowly disappeared from the sonar screen. Brice placed his finger on the fingerprint scanner on the drawer below the desktop. The drawer opened and he removed a special thumb drive. He inserted the drive and brought up an app. Nodded at Russell who got up and left the room.

Brice typed in a code and the information was integrated into a burst module. The icon showed the message was ready. He pressed the send icon. The burst was complete in four seconds. All went as planned. Brice shut down the equipment. If any ships or subs were lurking around their area, the two American destroyers would detect them and notify the Robertson. He would not have to sit and monitor the sonar screen.

MSS

The burst message arrived from their Embassy in Australia. The officer in charge copied the message to a thumb drive and handed it to his superior. Only his boss was allowed into the decryption room. He returned to his station.

The message was downloaded from the thumb drive into super secret decryption software. The MSS had only recently discovered the key to the American burst transmissions. The screen lit up. It was a message from a fleet in the south Pacific.

To: Vice Admiral Zimmerman
From: Captain H. Strong USS Cliptow
All is set. We have positive identification of the Chinese sub Fu Win. They most likely detected our fleet. We are prepared to take appropriate action on your orders.
Strong

The officer jerked as he read the message. He knew the Fu Win was the latest nuclear sub in the fleet and to be identified by the Americans was alarming especially if the unknown action should take place.

Another message had been received from the Fu Win by the clandestine group located several buildings away. Following protocol they released it to be added to the database. He immediately copied both messages into a secure server database. He removed the hot line phone from its cradle and spoke. "Sir, I have placed two very important messages we decrypted only moments ago into the database. I suggest you read Messages Number FW-897." He broke the connection.

Above the comms room a group of high ranking naval officers sat around a conference table. The Vice Admiral played the messages. They all looked shocked.

Fr: Science Officer Chi Lu Chong
The equipment is working as planned. We detected a large American fleet off the coast of Western Australia. We positively identified one nuclear battleship, two destroyers and many unknown signatures. Please advise.
End of transmission

The group sat very still. This was good and bad news. The secret equipment worked as planned, but the bad news was there is an American Fleet in Australian waters until now undetected. The Admiral stood. "How could that happen? How did the Fu Win get detected? We have spent a fortune on stealth hardware and software. We have satellite surveillance but none detected the American fleet. We have some very special equipment on the sub to be tested. It obviously worked. But if the Americans have identified the Fu Win, that means they had successfully captured its signature long before it reached Australian waters. That is unacceptable. We must plug that hole. Recall the Fu Win immediately."

The skipper of the Fu Win received the orders to return to China. Something was not right. No explanation was given.

Chong had just returned to his quarters when his inter com phone buzzed. The Captain informed him they were returning to base and broke the connection. When Chong checked in at 1700 all was well. Chong's handler did not mention anything about stopping the test. Chong went to the Comms room and sent a message to clarify what he was supposed to do. He got no answer back. This was most frustrating. The Captain gave no reason because most likely he didn't know either.

Canberra – Donovan

With breakfast done, Donovan and Rosenberg discussed the information received from McClusky. First they would find out if the Aussies have been notified. Donovan placed the call.

"Hello, this is Livingston."

"Mason, this is Donovan. Have you had any calls from McClusky in the last few hours?"

"No, I am not expecting any."

"Okay, I received one that I think I should make you aware of. Is now a good time to pop around?"

"Yes, please come straight away." Livingston hung up.

"Well, it seems McClusky did not call the Aussies. I think we should make them fully aware of all we know. If something goes sideways, at least we have not withheld any information." Tina nodded she was in agreement. They headed to the ASIO office.

Fifteen minutes later they were in the lobby showing their credentials. Livingston himself came to fetch them. Donovan explained that MI-6 had been contacted by someone using the code name Eye-in-the-sky. The message contained a photo of the assembly of the new nuclear sub. Livingston sat straight in his chair. His face did not reveal anything.

"Mr. Donovan, thank you for this information. When I told you we had uncovered a possible spy in the assembly building, I did not tell you we were monitoring all of his actions. That included his Facebook messages. We were aware he had taken a photo of the sub. What we don't know is how. Our best team watched his every move. No action could be detected that would result in taking a photo. They have eliminated the possibility of a second person. We are at a stalemate."

Tina leaned forward. "Sir, may we speak to your watch team?" Livingston stared at her for a few seconds. I'll have to get my superior to approve that request. They are in Adelaide. Are you willing to put off returning to the States?"

Donovan looked over at Tina. She nodded yes. "Sir, we are here to assist you. We are willing to put off our return to do that," said Tina.

Chapter Eighteen

Adelaide

The Qantas flight from Canberra was short. Tina and Mike deplaned and headed to the address they were given by Livingston. The taxi driver told them it was a twenty minute drive. Mike noted they were approaching the water front.

Tina paid the driver. Livingston had told them to ring the door bell twice. Mike pressed the button twice. The door clicked open. They went up the stairs to the second floor. Mike knocked on the door.

An attractive female welcomed them into the apartment. Sitting at a folding table was a young man who looked like he had been transported from San Francisco in the 60's. He had long hair, beard and clothes that would have been right at home in those days.

Mike introduced Tina and the female agent introduced the male as Freddy and she was Helena.

"Please have a seat. Can I get you anything?"

Tina smiled. "No thank you. I assume Livingston informed you we are assisting in the case."

Freddy nodded. "Yes he phoned a few hours ago. He told us that you were read in on what we have observed so far. We are stumped as to how the picture was taken and even more baffled as to how it got into his computer."

"Let's talk about that," said Tina. I've seen the photo. The angle of the photo is a bit strange. It appears to be taken from a low position, almost as if the photographer was seated on the floor."

Freddy looked over at Helena, "We thought we had an idea how the photo was taken, but it didn't turnout."

Mike looked concerned. "Did you report your suspicion?"

"Uh no. We concluded we were wrong and it was wishful thinking," said Freddy.

"What were your wishful thoughts?" asked Tina.

"We thought the camera was in his shoe. We watched the recording several times, but he never touched his shoe. The shoes were his street shoes and the only thing that he did not change before work. I can show you the recording," said Freddy.

Mike nodded yes. Tina and Mike watched the recording twice.

"Well, he definitely did not change his shoes. He crossed his leg while he sat waiting for his work partner. I didn't see him touch his shoes either. That doesn't mean he couldn't have used some remote device to snap the picture. Let's view the recording of him sitting outside the facilities again. Look for any movement of his hands."

The recording played again twice. "Nope, didn't move his hands in any way or any other body part," said Tina. They all sat in silence for a few moments.

"I have an idea," said Freddy. "Why not call for a security inspection, but have them move out to the hallway after removing their street clothes. We can then examine his shoes while they are out of the locker room."

"That's a great idea. Have Livingston call the N-5 security chief and explain we will be paying him a visit in the next hour." Mike noted the time was 1500.

"I can do that," said Helena. She picked up a cell phone on the table and made the call. She explained what was wanted with the security chief of the assembly building. She requested to have him meet the team outside the building's main entrance. She listened for a few seconds and punched off the call. "He is calling the security chief now. We can be at the building in ten minutes. I have a car parked on the street." Freddy shut down his laptop and motioned for all to follow him to the car.

On the short drive to the building, Freddy suggested he and Mike make arrangements to be already in the locker room at quitting time. They would need to wear a worker jump suit to blend in while the workers came into the locker room. As soon as they had removed their work clothes and shoes, the security chief would call the workers to the hall and close the door.

"That should work and give us more than five to ten minutes to examine the shoes," said Mike.

Helena parked the car in the visitor's area of the car park. A man in a uniform stood at the front entrance. As soon as they approached, he introduced himself as the security chief. Mike explained what they wanted. The man said nothing, just nodded he understood. He looked at his watch. "The shift will be over in ten minutes. This is a bit close but if we hurry, you can change into a work suit and be ready. They all walked swiftly down the hall and to the locker room. Mike and Freddy were handed the jump suits and saw Lee's locker as they walked down the row to two empty lockers with no names.

The chief returned to the hall and led Tina and Helena to an office where they could observe the locker room.

Mike removed his shirt and trousers and struggled into his tight jump suit. Freddy had already put his street clothes into an empty locker. Mike hung his street clothes and closed the locker door. They both sat down on a bench a few meters from Lee's locker.

There were three loud blasts from a speaker. The shift had ended. The workers would be arriving at any moment. Mike and Freddy turned and faced away from the incoming men. There was no chatter. Mike saw most of the men had removed their shoes and were putting their jump suites in their lockers when the Chief came in and ordered all to stop and follow him to the hallway. Mike and Freddy stood with all the men and pretended to move toward the hallway.

Freddy saw Lee's shoes sitting on the bench in front of his locker. The room door closed and they were alone in the locker room. Mike picked up one of the shoes and gave it a very close examination. Nothing. The second shoe was different. There was a small almost invisible hole in the toe. Mike put his hand into the shoe. "Bingo, the shoe is a camera. There is a fitting inside for a big toe to slide into. My guess is the big toe can move a certain way to trigger the mechanism. Look at this, it's a button built into the heel."

Freddy waved a device over the shoe. "It is a Blue Tooth transmitter. That's how he got the picture into his laptop. What now?"

"Nothing today. Let's discuss how this should be used," said Mike. "Let's get back into street clothes." They waited until the door opened and several men came back into the room. Lee sat on the bench and put on his shoes. He made no attempt to examine the shoes.

Tina watched Lee's every move. He was good. No attempt to examine his shoe for any tampering. Lee put on his shoes and closed his locker. He turned and looked briefly at Mike and Freddy who had their backs to him as they pretended to put on their shoes.

Mike saw Lee move toward the hallway and disappear with several others. "Let's get back to the apartment and see what he may have done today," said Mike. They met up with the security Chief, Tina and Helena in the hall.

No one spoke and the security chief walked with them to the front entrance. He nodded and left them as they exited the building.

A motorcycle moved by just as they came out of the door. The driver looked their way as he went by.

Observer's Apartment

The four were quiet as they climbed the stairs to the apartment. Freddy inserted his key and they all entered.

"Well, thanks to you Freddy, we now know Lee is our man and he has some very sophisticated equipment. Now the question is what do we do?"

Tina looked at Helena and Freddy. "Do you have the ability to fake his Facebook account?"

Helena had a surprised look on her face."Yes, we can clone his account and block his posts but make it appear as if it all worked. We've never done this, well officially, but it is possible. I have access to his router and can intercept and modify his incoming messages as well as outgoing."

"Great. If he received a message created by you to take a picture of a very specific area, and then we intercept his output message and put in our own picture in its place, we could control everything the MSS sees of the sub."

"Yes that is possible. We would have to have approval from our boss," said Helena.

They all sat silent for a few moments. "Is anyone hungry? How about a pizza? I'm buying," said Mike.

"There is a great pizza place just around the corner. I can phone in a delivery order. It should be here in less than forty-five minutes," said Freddy.

"No anchovies for me," said Tina. They all laughed. Freddy ordered a pizza supreme, no anchovies.

Helena opened her laptop and began to type in a message to Livingston. She motioned for Tina to observe. She wrote the details of how they could use the misinformation scheme. All pictures they inserted would be approved by Livingston's office. The MSS would see a bunch of phony pictures of a sub being built. Lee would not be aware his pictures were replaced with the phony ones. Mike read the message. "Perfect, Livingston should be thrilled, send it." Helena pressed the send button.

"Lee usually logs on to Facebook after his dinner, which is in about half an hour from now," said Freddy.

"Helena, you said you had access to his router. Can you intercept incoming Facebook messages and change the content and pass it on to appear normal?"

"The short answer is yes, but there will be a flicker when the message is released to his computer. Not something really noticeable but it is there. Changes to outgoing messages are not detectable, since we alter them after he hits his send button."

"Fine, I think we can live with that. What do we want to tell him to do?"

"Let's wait until we hear back from Livingston," said Mike. "We should wait to see what Lee's handlers have asked him to do."

The door buzzer sounded. The pizza was delivered. They all sat and enjoyed the pizza.

Right on time, Lee logged onto Facebook. There was no message. Freddy nodded at Helena. She logged into Lee's router just as a message popped up.

Take no more pictures until ordered to do so. Remain on the job.

Lee's response was a like.

The screen went to his screen saver. "Well that certainly changes things. Do you think somehow Beijing has discovered we found out about the shoe camera?" asked Tina.

"No, something else is in play. There appears to have been an event that has changed Beijing's focus," said Mike. He decided to phone Livingston himself and find out if they were privy to any major events concerning the Chinese.

Mike took out his phone and called Livingston.

"This is Livingston."

"Mason, this is Mike Donovan. I assume you received the message from your team. I have a question. Have your people received any alerts to a major event concerning the Chinese?" There was silence on the phone.

"Strange you ask that. We only moments ago intercepted a message from a Chinese Sub, the Fu

Win, that it had been detected. It was ordered to return to China. This is most unusual. As far as I know, we had no knowledge of the Fu Win being in Australian waters." Mike smiled. "Okay thanks Mason. We'll be leaving shortly. Your people are on top of the situation and everything is in good hands." Mike broke the connection. He pressed a series of numbers.

"This is Joker-1; I need to know your status." He listened for a several moments. Smiled and pressed the end button.

Everyone was looking at Mike. "Yep, there was something of an event concerning the Chinese. One of their top secret subs has been outed by the Aussies. It seems the sub was off the cost of Perth when detected. From the sudden halt of Lee's mission, they are uncertain as to what is going on. The sub hauled ass back to China. I bet there are a lot of people in Beijing trying to find a hole to crawl into." Helena and Freddy looked at each other.

"You guys have more tricks up your sleeve than a magician," said Helena.

We have a few other things to attend to, so if you can give is a ride to the airport, we'll get out of your hair," said Tina.

The ride to the airport was short compared to the route the taxi took. Some things are the same in any country.

Tina and Mike shook hands with Freddy, Helena had stayed back to monitor Lee.

As soon as they got their tickets, Mike and Tina sat in the waiting area of their gate. Tina looked at Mike. He looked back and started laughing. "I know, you are bursting to know what the hell the call was all about." Tina didn't laugh.

"Are you holding out on your partner?"

"No. This involves an operation that was launched before I got this gig. It is very involved and is classified. But, since the operation has begun, I feel I can bring you up to speed." He told her of the Robertson and how it has some extremely secret equipment to detect and deflect enemy ships and subs using a top secret database supplied by the US. "So how do you know what happened?"

"We have a man on board that is an observer. He was present when the sub was detected."

Is the Robertson a US vessel or an Aussie?"

She is in the Australian Navy and will play a major role in keeping the waters around Australia free of unwanted snoopers. Her sonar signature is brand new and not in any database. The Chinese will not know who she is."

"And how is all of that related to our mission?"

Mike stared into her eyes. "It's not, I think."

Chapter Nineteen

Langley Virginia

The CIA comms group received a message from the secret satellite network. It was quickly decoded and sent on to a section head. The message had identified a Chinese Submarine, the Fu Win. The section head entered the sub's signature and name into the top secret database. The information was beamed through a Pacific satellite to an Australian ship.

Fu Win

Chong sat in his quarters thinking about the short message from the Captain. He was concerned why he did not receive a reply from his handler. He decided not to send a follow-up message and would wait. As far as he knew everything had worked as planned. He would scan twice a day as ordered, even if the sub was headed back to China, and transmit at the appointed time.

MSS Beijing

A meeting had been called for all section chiefs to report to the conference room immediately. Eleven senior operatives along with all section chiefs sat silently waiting for the Minister to arrive.

The door banged open and one pissed off person stormed into the room. Everyone jumped at the entrance.

The Minister of State Security stood looking at the gathering. "Do any of you imbeciles know how an American fleet can go undetected and show up one-hundred nautical miles from our super secret submarine? How is it possible they know the name of the sub? I don't want speculation, I want facts."

The section chief for internal security raised his hand. "Sir, we detected a fishing vessel possibly using a satellite burst. They may have captured the Fu Win's signature when it left the base. The boat is being pursued at the moment. We will know the answer in a few hours." The Minister stared a long time at the section chief.

"How did a fishing boat get that close to the sub base? Have your people become so incompetent they ignore our basic protocols that prohibit any vessels within one-hundred miles of the sub base?"

"No sir. The boat was more than a hundred miles from the sub base. As soon as the ship was detected, it was pursued. It was disguised as an ordinary fishing vessel. But after the boat's crew realized they had been detected, it sped away at a speed far exceeding any of our patrol craft. The Air Service was notified to give assistance. They spotted the ship but it was heading into Vietnamese waters. We are continuing to pursue and have notified the Vietnamese we intend to pursue into their waters. They have acknowledged our request, but do not want the jets flying over their territory."

"You are telling me a boat more than one-hundred miles away was able to capture the signature of our sub? Is the bogus fishing boat Vietnamese? I want to be informed as soon as our people have caught the spy boat," said the Minister. The section chief nodded.

"What about our satellite surveillance system. It obviously failed to spot an entire fleet of American war ships. That is unacceptable."

"Sir, there seems to be an unknown problem with the satellite system. We still cannot find the fleet. Only a few scattered ships are showing up. Nothing like what the Fu Win reported seeing. I have checked everything. Our best systems people say the software is working. We can detect any ship within its scan window. The Americans may have come up with some type of stealth technology."

The Minister slammed his hand on the table. "I don't want any speculation, Stealth technology? This isn't Star Trek. If you can't solve the problem in twenty four hours, look for another job."

The operative handling the Fu Win special operation sat still. Sweat poured down his back. He looked down at the table top as the Minister looked around the table and spotted him.

"Moag, are you sure your equipment was working? Can you tell me without a doubt, the data was correct?"

"Yes sir, all is working as specified. We identified an American Battleship's nuclear signature and also the sonar confirmed the sighting. We know the battleship was the USS New Haven."

"What about your man, is he reliable?"

"Yes sir. He can collect the data but has no way to interpret or alter the results."

The Minister stared a full minute at Moag. The Minister turned and stormed out of the room.

The group looked at each other. They knew the Minister was ruthless and their jobs, maybe even their lives depended on them solving the surveillance problem. They slowly exited the room.

Vietnam

The disguised fishing boat made good time. A Chinese jet buzzed them twice. No doubt their location had been reported to the Chinese patrol boats. They were still an hour out from their home port. They could easily out run the patrol boats. As long as the jets stayed out to sea, they could disappear behind an island undetected. There were hundreds of small islands to hide behind.

Their home port was hidden by two large hills and a lagoon with two secret boat houses disguised as run down fishing shanties. Their boat could fit into either one. The shanties concealed large water filled caves into the hill. Each cave was large enough to house several boats the size of their vessel.

The leader on the boat aimed an infrared beam at a large rock sticking out from the mainland. It was a repeater and would relay his inferred message over land lines making the message undetectable. "This is Tan, we are coming in. We have been spotted. The patrol boats have not located us. We should be at the boat house in fifteen minutes. Tan out."

Fifteen minutes later, the fishing boat eased into the boat house and maneuvered into the cave. They tied up and unloaded the special equipment. The Sat dish was folded into the mast. All the other equipment was removed and put into the underground facilities.

John Watson smiled as his men came into the large room carved out of the hillside by eons of wave action. "Good job." He handed each a fat envelop. The American paid extremely well. It sure beat fishing. They all smiled and left for their homes.

Watson checked his messages. One from Langley had just arrived. He ran the message through his laptop decoding software.

The Fu Win is in the database. Good work.

The Chinese patrol boats scanned the coastal area of North Eastern Vietnam for hours. The fishing boat had disappeared among the hundreds of small islands. It could be anywhere. The jets could not fly close enough to get a firm location. They returned to their base.

Adelaide

Yen Lee fixed his dinner and watched the news on channel 7. The world was in a mess over the Covid crisis. So far as he knew, he had not heard of any cases at the ship yard. The vaccine and masks seem to be working. All employees had been vaccinated. The government was considering a lock down in Sydney, Perth, Melbourne and Brisbane. He knew it would be only a matter of days when it hit the entire country. There would be travel restrictions, closures of businesses and most entertainment venues would be affected. The public would be outraged.

Lee booted up his Dell laptop. He brought up Facebook. There was a notification indicating he had a Facebook message. He clicked on the messenger icon. There was a long message from Moag. He was ordered to find out if the American Fleet was still in the waters off of Perth. Lee reread the message.

How was he supposed to find out that kind of information? He deleted the message and sat thinking. His training as a MSS agent was limited to his mission, welding and taking pictures. He had no idea how to get Intel on an American Fleet. Lee typed a message to his handler.

I am not sure how to get your requested information. Please send me methods you recommend.
Yen Lee

Lee pressed the send button and the message was on its way. He knew the message would go to the Chinese Embassy in Canberra first before being sent to Beijing. He powered down his laptop and watched TV. He would check for any response first thing in the morning, before he left for work.

Above Lee's apartment, the two Aussie watchers had recorded his message from the MSS to find out about the American Fleet and his response. The messages were sent to Canberra.

Two men dressed in black slowly made their way to Lee's door. They inserted a key and opened the door. Lee was selecting a channel on his TV when he heard the door open. He turned as the silenced pistols coughed and deadly bullets entered his body. He was dead before his body hit the floor. The two men quietly closed the door and left the building.

Canberra ASIO

The message sent from the watchers in Adelaide was quickly decoded and sent to Mason Livingston's office.

Livingston read the messages. He was concerned. Somehow the Chinese had detected an

American Fleet off the coast of Perth. He had no knowledge of an American Fleet off the coast of Perth.

Livingston picked up his phone and called Mike Donovan. Mike answered and listened as Livingston read the messages. Mike told Livingston he was as out of the loop also. He had no knowledge there was an American Fleet in Australian waters, but he would make some inquiries and get back to him. Donovan told him the truth, there was no fleet.

Donovan and Rosenberg sat in the gate area waiting for their flight. Mike put away his phone and could not help himself, he laughed out loud. Tina looked at him for some sort of explanation

"It seems the Chinese detected an American Fleet off the coast of Perth and are in a tizzy fit. They have ordered our welder friend to find out the location of the fleet. The poor guy has no idea what to do. He asked for his handler to give him methods to go about finding out where the fleet is located."

Tina looked at Mike. "I'm lost, why is that so funny?"

"There is no fleet. The other part of my mission was to give the Aussies some secret technology that would make a snooping ship with sonar think there were many ships and actually have the signatures of real ships. It looks like they fell for it and are now trying to figure out why their surveillance satellite cannot find the fleet. I would think some heads will roll over this when they figure it out." The flight was called and they headed for the jet bridge to board their flight to Honolulu.

Just as he was reaching the jet bridge Donovan's phone beeped. He stepped aside and answered it. "This is Mike." He listened and frowned. Tina noticed his body language. Not good.

"Thanks for the info Mason. I'll be there shortly." Mike punched off the call. "That was Livingston. There has been a development with the watchers in Adelaide. It seems Yen Lee has been murdered. So far there are no suspects. They have asked for our help." Tina did not look happy.

"Well, what can we do? We're in a foreign country, no backup facilities and we don't even know who all the players are," said Tina.

Mike looked at her for a moment. "You can go on back. I'll stay and at show the Aussies we are willing to help."

Tina looked very uncomfortable. "I'd rather stay. At least we will have something to report. Are we to go to the ASIO, or straight to Adelaide?"

"I think we should go to Livingston's office and get as much info as we can. There might be something we can do to assist them." Tina nodded.

They told the gate agent they had revised their plans and would like to get their luggage off the plane. The agent smiled and asked for their tickets with the baggage tags. "The baggage has not been loaded yet so it will be no problem retrieving your bags. Would you like to reschedule your flight?"

"No not at this time. Can you just refund the ticket to our credit cards and then we will start over again when we firm up our plans," said Tina.

The agent smiled and entered data into her computer. "All is set. Your tickets have been refunded." The phone rang on her desk. She answered and listened. "Your baggage will be here in about ten minutes." Mike and Tina sat down in the empty gate area. After about five minutes a man with two bags entered through the jet bridge and sat the bags behind the counter. The agent checked the tags and brought the bags out to the waiting room area. "Are these the only bags?"

"Yes thank you very much," said Mike.

Mike and Tina were handed receipts for their refunded tickets and thanked the agent. They headed for the ground transportation area for a taxi to the Russell building not far from the commercial flight area.

Toulon, France

Kluso received a call to report to Navy head quarters immediately. He was not happy. It would take him more than an hour to make the trip. He wondered what could be so important to require him to personally appear in Toulon. He phoned his driver to bring the car around. Before he left for Toulon, he had one call to make. "This is Kluso, have you completed your part?" He listened. "Good. Check your bank account; the funds are on their way." He smiled and pressed the end button. The agent had done his job.

ASIO – Present time

Tina and Mike entered the lobby area and told the receptionist they had an appointment with Livingston. She phoned someone to escort them to Livingston's office.

Five minutes passed and Livingston himself came through the door and greeted the two. "Please follow me." The three went through to Livingston's office. Three men were seated in front of Livingston's desk. One was just completing a phone call and was putting his phone away. There were two empty chairs. Livingston pointed at the two empty chairs. Tina and Mike sat down.

Livingston introduced everyone. The three were his special ops section heads. They were put on the Lee case and were interested in what Mike and Tina could add to what they had already collected.

"Gentlemen, we interviewed your watchers and became involved in the case as it may affect the US's commitment to assist Australia to build its first nuclear submarine. We know Lee was a MSS agent in place and was assigned to take progress pictures of the sub. We also know he was ordered to find the location of an American fleet somewhere off the coast of Perth. I have checked with our people, there is no fleet off in Australian waters." The three sat listening and stared at Mike when he said there was no fleet.

Livingston nodded at one of his men. "Mr. Donovan, we have reliable sources that say there is a large fleet. One of the ships is the USS New Haven, a nuclear battle ship."

Mike smiled at the group. "Gentlemen, I repeat, there is no American fleet anywhere near Australia. The Chinese intelligence system may have picked up what they thought was a fleet with the New Haven but I assure you they were mistaken. I suggest you check with your own navy. I think they will verify what I have just told you."

Livingston picked up his phone. "Get me the Vice Admiral, priority one." He pressed a speaker button on the phone.

"This is the office of the Vice Admiral Mr. Livingston, He is unavailable but his assistant, Captain Thompson is available."

"Fine, put him on." A series of clicks and the voice boomed out of the speaker.

"This is Captain Thompson, how may I help you Mr. Livingston."

"Thompson, we have Intel that there is an American fleet with the battleship New Haven in the waters off of Perth. Can you confirm the Navy has detected this fleet?"

There was silence for a moment. "Sir, there is no American fleet in Australian waters." Livingston looked aghast.

"Thompson, why would the Chinese think there is an American fleet off the coast of Perth?"

Again silence on the line. "Sir, they most likely were mistaken. There are several classified operations going on at the moment that I'm not at liberty to discuss over open phone lines, but the Vice Admiral will be back tomorrow and I suggest you make an appointment to have a discussion with him. I can book you in at 0930 tomorrow morning."

Livingston was turning red. He was not accustomed to being put into a category of need to know. "Yes, that will be fine. I will be there at 0930." He pressed the off button and terminated the call. He stared at Donovan. "What is going on Donovan? Why was I not read in on this operation?"

"Sir, you will have to ask that question to the Admiral." One of the section chiefs spoke up.

"Mr. Donovan, I would like to remind you that you and Ms Rosenberg are guest in our country. I think it would be in your best interest to tell us anything you know about this fleet."

Tina looked at Mike, who smiled. "Mr. Atman, I am not a threat to Australia, just the contrary, we were sent here to look into how and why the AUKUS documents were leaked to the press. We are only here for that mission. If you feel we are interfering in your business, we will leave now." Mike made a motion to get up.

"Now, let's settle down, there is no need to get our feathers in a ruffle," said Livingston. "Atman, Donovan and Rosenberg are here to assist. So don't go on a witch hunt just yet. You heard Mr.

Donovan say, his mission is to investigate the leak of the AUKUS document. I personally confirmed that with Langley. Mr. Donovan, I apologize for any suggestion otherwise."

"Mr. Livingston, Mr. Atman, no apology necessary. We are all professionals and have to follow protocols. I understand your frustration. It appears things are occurring rapidly and you are in the dark. Believe me; I've experienced this type of situation many times. There are always classified programs to consider. The tighter the control over information has proven the higher the success rate." Atman reached over to shake hands. Mike took his hand and smiled as he shook his hand.

Mike turned to Livingston. "It seems the MSS wanted to eliminate any tracks back to them. They seemed to think Lee was expendable. None of this is involved in the document leak. We have concluded our investigation into the leak and have a very good idea how it was leaked and have concluded that the reason was to stir up resentment between pro French and the US and UK." Atman shifted in his chair and sweat broke out on his forehead.

Livingston stared at Mike. "When were you going to tell us your findings?"

That is not for me to provide. I report to Langley and Ms Rosenberg reports to NCIS in Washington. Our reports have been filed by us and you most likely will get a copy from our office in the next day or so."

Livingston nodded acceptance. "Can you hint at how this leak affected the building of the sub?"

"Personally, I don't think it will affect anything to do with the building of the sub, but it may impact certain agencies within your government."

Livingston looked shocked. "What was the reason for leaking such a document?"

"Sir, sometimes it is the most trivial of matters, in this case it led to an area we least expected and certainly confused us. That's about all I can say without breaking protocol."

"Well, thank you for being straight with us. It seems we have a lot of work on our end to complete. I am looking forward to getting a copy of your reports"

"Thank you Mr. Livingston. Ms Rosenberg and I will be spending the weekend in Sydney and then we will be leaving on Monday." Mike and Tina got up. Atman, one of the three section chiefs got up and volunteered to escort them to the front lobby.

"Hi, my name is Henry. It is my pleasure to show you back to the lobby. Sorry for the little ruckus." He opened the door and motioned for Tina and Mike to follow. They walked to the bank of elevators. Atman pressed the call button. The door opened and they boarded. He pressed the lobby button. As the car began to descend, he pressed the stop button.

"Sorry for this but I know you already know my role in the leak. I don't think you know why," said Atman."

Tina was surprised. "Okay, tell us what you think the reason was for the leak," said Tina.

"Several months ago I was approached by a French agent by the name of Kluso willing to pay a large amount to make the document public. My wife suffered from the Covid outbreak and nearly died. I needed money to pay for her long term recovery. Somehow he knew that I was in charge of placing the document in our archives. I was told to make a copy of the document and keep it to myself until further notice. I placed the copy of the document into my desk drawer and promptly forgot about it. From what I gathered from reading the document, there was nothing super secret. It only stated that the UK and USA were going to assist us in building a nuclear submarine. There was no mention of the French in the document. I was baffled why this was so important to Kluso. Several weeks ago, Kluso contacted me and told me to release the document to the BBC and CNN, which as you know I did. The reaction of the public to the release had its effect but, Kluso was disappointed. He wanted an uprising in our parliament to overturn the agreement between the UK and the USA. He came here to get Intel on the Chinese to be used to show the Chinese were involved. I don't know if he was successful. I never saw him and as far as I know he left the country."

"You haven't told us the reason for the release of the document," said Tina.

"Ms Rosenberg, all I was told by Kluso was the UK and the USA went behind their backs and took a very important project from the French. The country would lose a great deal of money and it would have a negative impact on their economy." Kluso told me the Australian government needed a diversion." He looked at Tina and shook his head.

"The Covid isolation was becoming a burden on the entire country. People were blaming the government. Mandatory restrictions were being put into place. The PM himself needed some diversion from the pandemic. Kluso touted that he knew what the PM wanted. He said the PM thought that if there was some event to divert people's concerns about the Covid thing, we could implement some sort of emergency controls and blame them on the event not the pandemic. Kluso said the AUKUS document would create a huge uproar, but no harm. It seems to have done its job. We have weathered the pandemic and the population has accepted the mandate as part of securing our secret data."

"Well Atman, you are correct. We guessed wrong. We thought the leak was to expose the UK and the US of clandestine maneuvering to oust the French contractors." Atman stared at Mike.

"Sir, that may have played a part in the reasoning but I assure you it was Covid that was the real reason." He pulled the stop button out and the car resumed its descent.

The door opened at the lobby level. Mike and Tina exited and turned to thank Atman. He had already walked away. "Wow that was rude. Do you believe his story?"

"No, but he did give me a hint of the real reason. When I told him what we thought, I saw his eyes widen. I had hit on the reason. He tried to move us back to the Covid reason. Not good enough. I think Mr. Atman is working for the French and it was them that created this whole panic. The leak itself was a no event. The press gave it a small play then after the second day it disappeared. I think they knew it was a plant for some political purpose. The French were pissed at the UK and the US for taking their lucrative contract. Atman's Covid thing just didn't sound realistic. The average Aussie just shrugged at the entire AUKUS thing. They still focused on the government as the scapegoat for the miserable way the Covid thing made their lives. When in doubt, blame the government."

Tina looked at mike as they walked to the taxi stand. "What about Atman? If he is a French agent, then should we tell Livingston?"

"When he gets my report, he will know. Before I was sent here on this case, I was briefed by the section chief in charge of the secret decoy system for the Australian Navy. They had come across Atman's communications with Kluso. We knew he was a French agent reporting to Kluso. I asked if I should read you in on that case since it was somewhat involved in the leak. My boss felt Kluso's clumsy attempt to involve the Chinese was not for us to get involved in. We did not want to expose that information but thought we could feed misinformation. We never got the chance to do that. It seems Kluso failed to create the up roar he wanted.

"Thanks for clearing that up. I've enjoyed working with you. I've learned a lot. Maybe we will be paired up again." Mike smiled as he got into the taxi.